The Renter

Other books by Michael Tregebov

The Briss
The Shiva
Shot Rock

MICHAEL TREGEBOV

The Renter

a novel

VANCOUVER
NEW STAR BOOKS
2021

 NEW STAR BOOKS LTD

No. 107–3477 Commercial St., Vancouver, BC V5N 4E8 CANADA
1574 Gulf Road, No. 1517 Point Roberts, WA 98281 USA
newstarbooks.com · info@newstarbooks.com

The publisher acknowledges the financial support of the Canada Council
for the Arts, the British Columbia Arts Council, and the Government of
Canada.

Cataloguing information for this book is available from Library
and Archives Canada, www.collectionscanada.gc.ca.

Cover design by Oliver McPartlin
Typeset by New Star Books
Printed and bound in Canada by Imprimerie Gauvin, Gatineau, QC

First printing February 2021

Adieu to Benny,
Bonjour to Liam

Why have pleasure when you can have pain?
Catullus, by Pawel Eisner

ONE

In July 1960, while Bret Yeatman's dad lay dying of kidney cancer, his mother Sally rented a small cottage from Shecky Kaufman for six weeks on Ash Avenue in Winnipeg Beach, on Lake Winnipeg. It had a screened in veranda sagging off the front room where Bret, 12 at the time, and his brother Carl, only 10, played Monopoly when it rained. From that day forward, Bret made a promise to God that he would one day buy her a cottage of her own. He believed in that promise as much as he believed in the God he made it to.

Bret's dad, Morris, was against the idea of renting the cottage, but Sally Yeatman had saved up the money from her job selling perfume at the Hudson's Bay Company, and by the time Morris was admitted to hospital, he had given in. It would be better, he told Sally, for the boys to be at the lake than watch him deteriorate in the hospital. Their mother had managed to dissemble so well that Bret and his younger brother Carl weren't even aware that their father was dying.

If Bret had to choose one thing he loved his mother for, it would be that summer. From the day they moved into the cottage, he was intoxicated by the strangeness of Winnipeg Beach. He awoke to mornings on which the early sun made the grass and rushes steam in an ode to evaporation and the air fill with the smell of tar-sprayed streets and split maples and oaks dripping sap. Within days, his blond hair went blonder and his skin tanned quickly.

His mother gave him and Carl extra allowances to buy comics at McGregor's Drugstore. They spent mornings reading comics there and every evening he rode his bike back and forth from the Point, north on Prospect Road to Sandy Hook, the setting sun warming his shirt, past beautiful cottages and intermittent thickets. When he felt like it, he'd ride down the narrow wooden piers off Poplar Street and the odd-numbered avenues and watch flocks of American white pelicans land along the shore that curved southeast to the water tower and northwest to Gimli.

That summer, he and Carl made four phone calls to their father in the hospital, from the payphone outside McGregor's. When it was Bret's turn to talk, he'd tell his father about the cottage and the beach and his bike rides. One day he asked his father if he was going to drive up the next week. His father said he couldn't make it next week, but didn't explain why.

– Are you getting better? Bret asked him on the last call.

– They're giving me a special treatment. Should be good as new. I promise.

– I'll take the Saturday morning bus into town to visit, Bret offered. – I promise too.

His father hesitated.

– Taking the bus alone? Maybe you shouldn't. I … I think you have to be a certain age.

Shecky Kaufman came to collect the rent on the last day of their stay. Normally, Sally Yeatman demanded respect from everyone, but that afternoon, she was almost obsequious to Shecky. Upset by this change in her behaviour, Bret rode hard that night, all the way out to the northernmost pier. The setting sun shimmered red above the lake, making the sweep of the lakeshore more poignant, the air sweeter, and the clouds over the lake. He got off his bike at the head of the pier and began wheeling it down.

That's when he saw her: a girl with long dark hair, compact breasts and legs tanned a golden brown, wheeling her bicycle up the pier towards him. They passed awkwardly at the point where the pier narrowed to no more than a yard. The spruce two-by-sixes beneath drooped and cracked in a miniscule but regular rhythm until the moment Bret's tires rubbed hers, making them both stop.

– This is a private pier, she said.

– Is it your private pier?

– Maybe.

– Can I stay a while?

– Maybe.

– What's your name?

– Sandra. Yours?

– Bret.

– Are you Jewish?

– Yes.

– Hmm. Maybe you are.

He reflected on the fact that, although Jewish, he was estranged from the community. His father had lost his door factory five years earlier after being swindled by two builders, Eddie and Dave Gilman, who had reneged payment on a monstrous order, which his father said he delivered to the last doorknob. Morris had borrowed to cover his negative cash flow, but, eventually, the debt dug a hole down into which went: the factory, then their savings, then their house in River Heights, then their friends, then his father's health. They were forced to move back to the North End, their lives eroding at both ends.

His mother now had only one Jewish friend left, Mona Joffe, their neighbour. They had even been dropped from membership at the synagogue because they could no longer pay the dues, which meant that Bret hadn't been bar mitzvah'd, which was a relief for him but a torment for his father. The Jewish Child and Welfare Services had paid for Bret and Carl to go to the YMHA on Saturdays – to breathe Jewish air – but his father's reversal of fortune meant that they were virtually ignored there, sometimes vexed.

– *Ech*, she said, rolling her shoulders just as thunder rolled under distant clouds and the setting sun made one side of her face glow red.

That's when he remembered seeing her at the town arcade from time to time with a small band of girlfriends who were always barefoot: an odd sign of their affluence. He remembered fantasizing what it would be like to be admitted into their company.

– Are you a renter? Sandra asked.

– Yes.

– So you don't own your cottage?

– Would we rent if we did? Is that your cottage? he asked pointing his chin towards a large lakefront place with a sleek lawn, a screened-in veranda and a deck, more a house than a cottage because it was winterized and had a cement foundation.

– Maybe, she said.

– And this really is your own pier?

– Maybe.

– If I let you kiss me, he said, would you let me sit on your pier till it gets dark? It's my last day.

– Why do you think I'd want you to kiss me?

– Do you?

– Maybe.

– Why do you say 'maybe' to everything? he asked.

– It's a kick. Just a kick with me and my friends. Maybe means 'yes.'

– It's annoying.

– You want that kiss or not?

– Maybe, he said.

– But only because it's your last day, she said.

She nodded and together they wheeled their bikes down the pier towards the lake, she wheeling backwards with hers. They leaned them against the handrails, his against hers, entangling the spokes. When Bret realized she was going to keep her promise; he felt that deep inside she had generous feelings.

She sat down on the top step of the soggy wood staircase that led down into the lake, and patted the spot beside her. He sat, and they positioned themselves for kissing.

– Close your eyes. Don't look at me. I'm shy, she said.

He squeezed his eyes closed, and she opened his lips with her lips while touching his neck with her fingertips. Her tongue slipped between his teeth, reaching deep inside to lick his palate. She's kissed guys before, he thought. Their kiss lasted twenty minutes but it was still over too fast. He felt that her kiss had just transformed life, made it nice to be alive.

When he opened his eyes, the sun had set and the clouds were pulled taut, darkening the sky, making the faery lights that garlanded the elms on her front lawn and the posts of the pier flicker and burn.

– I've got to go, she said, nodding toward her cottage. – Important guests are coming if they've turned all the lights on.

The next day Bret, his mom, and Carl, packed up and drove

home. They were going straight to the hospital, which is the last place Bret wanted to go.

– Is he going to be okay? Carl asked, as they drove past the last wheat field before the outskirts of Winnipeg.

– The doctor says he'll be fine, his mother said, in her hide-the-truth voice.

– He's still going to recover? Bret asked.

– Fully, Sally said.

– You're not hiding anything?

– There's nothing to hide.

Bret rode the rest of the way back to Winnipeg, enjoying the wonderful expectation of his father's recovery. But one look at his father in the hospital bed, and Bret realized that his mother was right, in a way. There was nothing to hide: his father's deterioration, his posture, his smell crushed him.

Bret realized then that he hadn't thought of his father much that July. And he had broken his promise to take the Saturday morning bus into town to see him because he had preferred to read comic books. He would have to make a new promise, this time to keep his father alive.

Two days later, before he could come up with the right promise, Bret watched his father die after one last gasp to try and suck in more life. He watched his mother weep as an orderly wheeled his father's body into the corridor and parked it against the pale green wall. Bret's heart shattered and, to dull the pain, he told himself that what he was experiencing was just a dream. He shut his eyes tightly against the roaring of the hospital noises and his mother's sobs and willed himself to never open them again.

TWO

W hen he opened his eyes again it was early morning on a hot July day in 1968. He was 20 and back on the pier where a girl named Sandra had let him kiss her eight years earlier. Although he had dreamt of it, he had not been back to Winnipeg Beach in all that time. Their poverty, which had at first inched up on them during the debt years, had gripped their throats when his father died; his father's war pension was halved, and his mother went on welfare, which made renting a cottage ever again hopeless.

Before he had driven out, Sally had asked him to buy a *yahrzeit* candle for the eighth anniversary of his father's death. It was a full month away but she had grown cautious about not doing things right away, for she feared it could lead to not doing things at all.

He rented a cottage from Shecky Kaufman with bonanza money he'd made selling marijuana; the end of the school term was good for business. It was a fair chunk, and with it he could have put a down payment on a small cottage for his mother or given her a holiday somewhere else: she'd always wanted to see the Rockies. He really did like the idea of buying a cottage but he didn't follow through. Instead, he banked some of the profits, held a lot in cash, and invested the rest in new supply.

It had been impossible to rent the same cottage they'd had eight years earlier, but he found another one on Ash, closer to the beach and the town. The front yard had two fencerows of unkempt lilac bushes and was spotted with birch and ash trees and a blighted elm that was already shedding yellow leaves.

Many cottages at Winnipeg Beach had family names or funny names that suggested family names. His cottage was named *Winners*, a jovial representation of the Winograds. The name had been burnt into a flat piece of driftwood and spiked into a large tree in the front yard. If this were his cottage, he mused, he would be practical and put up a sign simply saying *The Yeatmans* or, more extravagant and satisfying, *Villa Sandra*.

The cottage had indoor plumbing and running water, and a newly fitted kitchen, although the old rainwater cistern under the eaves was still hooked up to a single steel tap that gaped into a zinc tub in the screened-in back veranda, which had a door that faced west and let you out into the backyard. The veranda walls were clad in white-washed spruce planks and the white floorboards creaked authentically. He promised himself he would sleep there, the very first night on the wicker daybed, so he could hear the sloshing of the waves on the shore.

That first evening, after baking on the beach, and following that up with a long cold swim, he looked at his kitchen door which top to bottom was filled with a large red sun and enjoyed its warmth. On the opposite wall, a round kitchen mirror caught the sun's reflection just as Smokey Robinson and The Miracles' 'I Heard It through the Grapevine' came over his transistor radio. He'd heard the new Marvin Gaye version earlier that year and couldn't decide which one he liked better. He was stripped to the waist, having just rinsed his hair in the zinc tub using the rainwater tap. He combed it and then shaved carefully around the burns before giving his face a final scrub with rainwater.

Spruced up, he put on a laundered short-sleeved white shirt

and felt as cool as Smokey Robinson. He was expectant about what the summer might bring. He went to the kitchen cupboard to see what Shecky's last tenant may have left behind and found a twenty-dollar bill in a butter dish. Out of curiosity, he wondered what might be in the fridge. It was dark inside, and when he plugged it in and opened the egg compartment, he found a five-dollar bill to cap his luck.

He got his bike out of the trunk of his used 1960 Ford Falcon, oiled the chain and sped off to re-visit the scenes of his first summer eight years earlier. On First Avenue near Prospect he noticed a 'For Sale' sign on a picket pounded into the lawn of a cottage. He memorized the number and promised himself he'd phone the next day and see if he could make a dent in that promise he'd made to his mother so long ago.

Under a deep pink dusk he pedalled leisurely to the pier where Sandra had kissed him. Renovations had been made: there was a large, freshly varnished platform, to which a small rowboat was moored. From the head of the pier he saw a party going on at her cottage – if it was still her cottage – about sixty kids laughing and drinking. Like the twenty-dollar bill in the butter dish and the fin in the fridge, the party made him happy, it seemed to be another sign of good luck. So he decided to crash it.

He rode back down the pier and onto Prospect, gliding down the cottage private driveway till he got stuck in gravel. Two boys standing in the gravel stared at the back of the cottage. Bret could tell they hadn't been invited and were staring at their own exclusion. He leaned his bike against a birch tree and walked across the carport and through the screened-in porch and into the kitchen. Off the counter he grabbed a can of beer and entered the front room, alert, his heart pounding, in the hope of seeing Sandra. He recognized no one, but if she had changed as much as he had, would he recognize her? There were two plump girls giggling in cut-offs, bare knees up to their chins, pushing their eyeglasses up the bridges of their noses, but he glided past them, sipping his beer as he passed through the front screened-in veranda off the living room and went out the door someone had left open. He loped down across the lawn toward the pier. The whole circle he'd just made took less than two minutes but he'd not seen Sandra. It occurred to him suddenly that her parents may have sold the cottage.

He walked all the way down the pier and sat down on the platform beside a lone girl smoking a cigarette. She wasn't Sandra, but the way she dangled her naked tanned feet into the lake made his face hot.

– Can I sit here? he asked.

– Free country, she answered, flicking her cigarette into the lake.

Despite the muggy night, she was wearing an expensive-looking red cashmere sweater on top of a white blouse. Her frayed white cut-offs covered just inches of her round thighs. She wore a thick gold charm bracelet on her left wrist. He felt sexual good fortune under his skin when she finally smiled up at him. She had dark eyes and full lips.

– Something tells me you weren't invited here.

– I was just riding by.

– Every party needs a party-crasher.

– I once met the girl whose family owned this cottage.

– Sandra Sugarman?

– Are you a friend of hers?

– Cousin. I'm the summer guest. Liz Kowtun.

– Bret. Bret Yeatman.

He removed his canvas sneakers, sat next to her, and dangled his feet into the lake too. He took a sip from his beer can, wiped the lip of the can and offered it to Liz. She waved it away with a petite hand with closely clipped fingernails.

– Do you have a boyfriend? he asked.

– Here?

– Anywhere.

– I'm from out of town. Toronto.

– Do you have a boyfriend in Toronto?

– I have a *not-a-boyfriend*. Do *you* have a boyfriend?

He'd have to be sharp now, too, he thought.

– You're not very nice, he said. Did anyone ever tell you that?

– I'm nice for Toronto. Do you go to university?

– Sure, Bret lied. I go there a lot.

From her self-confidence, the cashmere sweater, the sandals, and the gold bracelet thick as a lariat, he figured: rich Toronto girl. His imagination rushed ahead, the attraction turning venal. Why not? he thought. She'd have no chance against him. They'd get emotional, and emotion led to sex. Sex would convert to infatuation, and infatuation to love. She'd be no match because he was a natural, and he was a natural because he enjoyed love. Maybe one day he could even explain his venality to her and she'd laugh.

Marrying money was an option like any other, and he was a bit surprised that he had never thought of it before. There were precedents. His mother knew several athletic and smooth boys without a pot to pee in from Stella Avenue who'd married up. She called them zipper-marriages. Why not him? He'd be able to catch up to everyone else. He couldn't sell grass all his life, could he?

The rush of his imagination towards advantageous matrimony now acquired the quality of work and suddenly he couldn't think of anything to say.

In the water, kids were slipping their bathing trunks down their thighs, mooning anyone watching, but mostly each other. The lake water amplified their screams and laughter.

– There's a full moon, Liz said, pointing at the wet bum of a fat kid.

– That's funny, he said.

– A laugh would have been more genuine.

– You're funny.

– For Winnipeg, she said, with superiority. Do you want to see something? Something really something.

– What?

She picked up her sandals and took his hand and led him off the pier to the pine and glass gazebo change-house at the shore that hadn't been there eight years earlier.

The moonlight reflected green and silver off the sliding doors facing the lake. Trying to stifle his excitement, feeling her squeeze his hand, all of a sudden seducing Liz Kowtun didn't seem like work at all. They couldn't see inside until they cupped their temples to the glass to pry. It was pitch black inside, and he anticipated seeing the 'something' Liz had mentioned.

What he saw once his eyes adjusted was a girl naked from the waist up sitting on a boy with his shirt open. He saw another girl with a sundress rumpled around her midriff. He made out five couples in all, dry humping or necking on the rugs and chester-fields to the music of Buffalo Springfield's 'For What It's Worth.' They were like sweet animals, he thought. Liz Kowtun squeezed his hand again.

Suddenly, more than Liz he desired the cottage itself: its decks and verandas, and the ample lawns that sloped gently down to this pine and glass change-house gazebo with the kids inside, and farther off a pine boathouse – also new – jutting out over the lake. His life suddenly felt suffused with a sense of purpose he had never experienced before. It was his turn to squeeze Liz's hand, which he did until it hurt her.

– Now what? he asked.

– Let's go to the movies? That's what couples do when they don't know what to do.

– Really?

– I'm kidding. Look at those two.

– Which ones?

– She's on top of him. Sanding against the grain.

He had a certainty: in a minute she would kiss him, maybe ask him to make love with that kiss. He wanted to save her the embarrassment and pulled one of his favourite lines out of his hat.

– If I let you make love to me, do you promise not to fall in love with me?

– Do you promise to withdraw? I can't get pregnant in Winnipeg.

– If that's what you want, he said, forgetting her name suddenly, wondering how he'd remember it.

– You're beautiful, she said, kissing him. I've never seen a boy as beautiful as you.

If he got her pregnant, he thought, she would have to marry him. Could it be that easy? Would her family have the equivalent of these possessions in Toronto, but on a Toronto scale?

– Let's go in, she said.

– There's a dozen people inside.

– But there's room on the floor by the fridge, she laughed.

– Can't we go somewhere alone? To your bedroom?

– No. Where then? Boathouse?

– Done it there before?

– I just got here today.

– What will you tell your 'not-a-boyfriend'?

– There is no 'not-a-boyfriend'. God, you're dim.

The night was beautiful, his heart was high, and he wanted to celebrate both. He grabbed her by the waist with one arm and didn't let her go until they were inside the boathouse, the screen door on a tight spring clapping shut behind them. Inside, it was high-raftered and smelled of sawed wood. Canoes and oars hung from opposing walls, and a wooden inboard gently bobbed on lake water, making sucking and slapping sounds. Against the back wall there were retired golf bags and clubs and a large veal-coloured leather couch. He felt the luck trapped under his skin mingle with the liquid warmth of the sun that had roasted him on the beach in the afternoon. And now he was breathing deeply.

– You've got a winter boner, she said.

– I can do better. You're beautiful.

– You don't have to butter me up. Hey, you're circumcised. I didn't think you would be. I didn't think you were Jewish like me. Do you know what Toronto telepathy is?

– No.

– Put your hand behind my neck. Just one hand. Now I'll do the same.

He felt her long hair under his fingers as he squeezed her by the nape, and then the heat of her hand going through his collar. His whole body shivered.

– Now press your forehead into mine. Firm, but it shouldn't hurt.

– Okay.

– Now I'll send you a thought, and you tell me what it is.

– I know it.

– I haven't sent it yet. Just wait. Close your eyes.

He waited for her to dispatch her thought and he wondered what to invent, whether to be funny or romantic. After a minute, she released him.

– What was it? she asked.

THREE

Bret woke up first. Liz slept on in a darkness drilled by narrow sunbeams. He got up and opened the inside door and was dazzled by yellow sunlight glancing off the stones and the sand and through the mesh of the screen door.

The lake was flat, and a pelican bobbed upon the molten shimmer of the water. A robin, perched on a nearby lilac bush, chirped and then changed branches. He heard and saw two dragonflies buzzing the dandelions. There was a pageantry to the warmth beyond the screen: such wonderful things had not happened to him for a long time and he got the feeling that even something better was blooming.

He looked back at Liz Kowtun, breathing effortlessly as she slept on the cracked leather couch that had served as their bed. Her skin was evenly tanned and spotless, her glossy black hair looping the breasts he had squeezed until she had slapped his fingers saying 'that's not what turns me on'. Her face was not as beautiful though. Perhaps it was his assessment that had diminished her looks, or maybe it was the guilt he always felt after making love.

When he turned back to the door he saw a tall, lithe girl with long, thin brown hair and a prominent nose making a beeline toward the boathouse, maybe to take out the inboard or one of the canoes hanging on the wall. He recognized her unmistakably as the girl who had kissed him for twenty minutes eight years ago. Sandra Sugarman had matured well.

The closer Sandra got, the more his heart pounded. He'd thought he had become fearless through his years of dealing but now he remembered what it was like to be scared. Certain that Sandra had not seen him standing at the screen door, he snuck back to the couch to shove nimbly against Liz from behind her so that if Sandra walked in she would see them like that.

Bret, in the semi-darkness, could make out Sandra, her hands cupping her face against the screen to see in. For eight years her face had been both refuge and fantasy for him: there were no other real or imaginary faces that could compete with its power over his psyche. And now seeing it spy at him through the screen, he saw a different face, one more real than the face he had had to invent and reinvent until it eventually bore little resemblance to the original.

Liz Kowtun's body stretched and curled and shunted itself peacefully back and forth into Bret's abdomen as he stroked the front of her thighs from behind. Liz's throat burbled. He saw how she coloured at the neck expecting his hands to move higher up. Sandra, he noticed, took her time staring at their slow-moving bodies before walking away.

– Was someone at the door? Liz asked. Did someone see us?

– Don't panic, Bret said, nudging her bum.

– You're lying. How long were they watching?

– A while.

– I lied, too. I actually do have a 'not-a-boyfriend.' He humiliated me, but I didn't break up with him. Could you tell?

– What?

– That I lied about him?

– Why?

– I bet you it was Sandra at the door. Breakfast time. She was probably looking for me. Did she see us, you think? She was humiliated, too, you know. A guy dumped her. It's a real shock when it happens; in fairy tales, the guy is a prince. I was brought here to commiserate with her. It was worse for her because she was engaged. To Steven Bilinkoff. You know him?

– Was he here last night?

– Doubt it. He thought he could do better than her. You can go in all the way if you want. Just don't come inside. She got panic attacks from the disgrace, mostly in the car when she drove, and now she depends on people to chauffer her where she needs to go, although she's always felt people were here to serve her. Are you sure she's gone? I'm close if you don't stop.

– I won't.

– There I go, she said, and wet the couch.

Bret couldn't believe his good luck: with an adoring gaze, Liz Kowtun and her cashmere sweaters, every evening a different colour, tied around her narrow waist, followed him around town, from Dorothy's Chips to the Playland arcade or from cottage parties to beach bonfires. Gone was her clever sarcasm. On Liz Kowtun's insistence, and Sandra's say so, Bret was indulged by Sandra's clique, where he enjoyed being the outsider allowed in, where just his presence, he thought, was his conversation.

There was one guy in the group, Danny Shnatz, who didn't recognize him, or pretended not to recognize him from the YMHA years ago. Danny's younger brother, Eddie, was a prick: mean in the way rich kids are mean, and had done something to Bret not easily forgotten. In front of Danny, too, who was pretty normal compared to Eddie.

After being ignored at the YHCA for a year, 15-year-old Bret managed to make it into a clique that Eddie led because Bret had become skilled at floor hockey, and Eddie wanted him for his team. Bret played hockey and hung around with those kids for over a year and thought he had gotten close to Eddie. They'd even had a malt together in the Eaton's basement, with Danny tagging along. Then, out of the blue one Saturday afternoon, after Y, a dozen kids were hanging around on Hargrave Street waiting to go to a party for which he had made his mother buy him a new shirt she couldn't afford. Suddenly, Eddie called Bret a mooch, a leech, and a suck hole, in front of everyone.

Bret's skin began to burn with shame, until red patches flowered on his cheeks and neck.

Then a friend of Eddie's wiped his palm on Bret's arm, turned and wiped it on the back of another kid in the clique and said:

– Now you've got Yeatman's germs.

Bret was stunned; the expression was cruel and perverse and everything evil in the world was compressed into it.

The kid, whose back had been wiped, then wiped his hand on another kid's sleeve and said: You've got them now. Bret's germs were passed from kid to kid, they played tag with them, panting with fun. Danny couldn't hack what was happening and had started bawling.

To make matters worse, Eddie had ended by telling the other kids that Bret was only a member of the Y because the Jewish Child and Family Services were paying. To the kids who couldn't draw their own conclusions, Eddie explained that Bret's family couldn't afford the membership.

A chorus of three mean voices struck up a call:

– Suck! Suck! Suck!

Eddie was nothing if not relentless and wouldn't stop until the entire pack of kids hounded Bret all the way up Hargrave Street shouting: Suck! Suck! Suck! He'd stop every few steps and glare at them, but they'd advance again and continue the torment.

To escape the squealing and shrieks, Bret broke into a run and did not stop to look back until he crossed Portage Avenue against a red light to the stop in front of Eaton's where he always caught the Templeton bus home, all the while thinking that he had deserved what had just happened to him because he had neglected his father the summer he died.

He had dealt with his father's death by convincing himself it was all a dream; he'd extended the same process to this crushing disgrace. It was all just a dream, and the affluence of Eddie Shnatz and friends was a dream too. Rich kids like Eddie were only dreaming they were rich and had power over him. It was a useful philosophy, on which he sometimes cheated: he also thought that his good luck could be real.

Afterwards, his social worker from Jewish Family Services, Zev Moss, was kind enough not to force him to go back to the YMHA. He spent weekends alone after that, skating at Kildonan Park or watching TV with his mother and Carl: *The Man from U.N.C.L.E.*, *Mission Impossible* and *Man in a Suitcase*, or sometimes a *Wayne and Shuster* special or a *Juliette* special, which made him nauseous with frustration.

His emancipation from the Y led him to accept the offer Mona Joffe's son, Duddy, made to introduce him to Max Shanus, a criminal lawyer, who'd defended Duddy in court for kicking many living daylights out of a guy at the stockyards during a strike. Max Shanus also ran an import-export business in Chinatown, above his father's pawnshop, and was also involved in drug dealing with Morris Greene.

Max Shanus was a pot dealer of some importance in Winnipeg. He wore his prematurely grey-blond hair long and tucked behind his ears, so it was impossible to figure out his age. He was as easily 30 as 45. And he liked mod shirts with long collars, but he didn't wear jeans.

It was Max who set Bret up selling nickel bags on Saturdays in front of the Timothy Eaton statue on the main floor of Eaton's. Max said it was his start in life, where, sipping on a chocolate malted, Bret kept his eyes peeled for narcs, easily spotted because they looked too crabby for their hippy duds.

Bret began to realize that the only good thing about the YMHA had been the floor hockey and the chips with gravy they served in the restaurant. He did miss those chips, but the money from dealing compensated for that and the razzing and disgrace on Hargrave, while the heartbreak of having no friends had taught him a dirty thing about life.

He remembered his first payment to Max Shanus for fronting him the plastic bags of pot, always wrapped in Perth Cleaner's laundry parcels and delivered using a dead drop system. They'd been sitting in the Paddle Wheel restaurant at The Bay, at a table next to the replica of a steamer's paddle wheel churning the water in the large flat wishing well where little kids tossed in pennies and nickels and made wishes.

Bret was nervous, and awestruck to be meeting Max in person; he'd figured Max would send one of his 'gophers' or 'camels' or 'sliders' that Bret dealt with.

– How'd it go with you? Max asked him.

– Sold it all.

When Bret pulled out a purple velvet Seagram's bag from a concealed pocket in his parka lining, he felt he was holding a pouch of gold dust for Max to see.

21

– You keep your money in that? Max asked. – I kept marbles in a bag like that.

– This is my marble bag.

– Still got them?

– I kept my best ones. The others I gave away. I had a thousand when I was a kid. Alleys and crocks. Duddy gave me his old collection.

– Duddy'll give anybody anything, Max said.

– How do you do it? Bret asked. You're a lawyer and a businessman and all this too? Duddy says you live in a mansion on West Gate.

– Don't believe Duddy when he talks.

– No. Really. Tell me. How?

– Brains and personality, said Max. – Brains and personality. Bret slid the pouch over to Max.

– Hefty. Are you paying me in marbles?

Max loosened the gold cord of the Seagram's pouch, took out his cut and pulled the cord. Bret had thought Max was going to take a bigger cut than he did, and he didn't know if Max was being generous or not.

Sure, now he had extra money to give to his mother and Carl. He thought maybe he'd just buy books and comics for Max and groceries or clothes for his Mom. Not hand her cash. At least for now. That way he could avoid explanations, but he didn't know what to say if she asked him how he'd come by any of it, so he asked Max what he should say.

– Tell her you do import-export work for Max Shanus on Saturdays. Everybody knows me. Are you still in school?

– I dropped out when I turned 16.

– New life?

22

– New nothing.

– No Jewish friends?

– Nothing.

– I'm your friend, Max said.

It was true. Bret had no Jewish friends, except Max, who didn't count because he was an adult. He did hang out with young pushers, most from failing homes, who were not inclined to humiliate each other verbally. Instead, they just slugged each other and got slugged back. They had small bands of teen girls to play with: girls who varnished their nails, wore heavy eye shadow and lipstick, but were submissive despite looking tough.

Now, in Winnipeg Beach, it was strange to be back in a Jewish clique, where the girls didn't paint their nails, wore no make-up, and where the boys felt comfortable with criticizing you and being criticized.

He had fun sometimes with the boys. They'd go for moonlight swims and they'd do that Chinese fire drill thing, stopping the car in the middle of traffic: everybody jumping out, running around the car, changing places. It got old quickly but it was fun at first to share the hilarity.

In all, Bret's life was certainly sweet those first two weeks of summer: Liz Kowtun, who had started off being sharp and sarcastic on the pier that first night, had now become as sweet in conversation as she was warm and pliant and easy to satisfy in bed. Bret thought at times that he might have to prevent her from kissing his feet, and eventually found her fawning annoying. He was worried that he was getting tired of her, like he had with the other girls who varnished their nails and wore eye shadow.

Then Liz started wearing lipstick. The fact that she was the only girl in the clique who wore lipstick cheapened her for him. But whenever he mentioned to her how she had changed, in an attempt to change her back, she bridled and grew sharp again, which rekindled her appeal.

On the nights he was critical with her, she took her time making love, happy with satisfaction, so naturally endowed was she for sucking in pleasure just by being held and stroked, or even just from having her hair smoothed off her forehead, which he enjoyed as much as getting off. They also played Chinese checkers afterwards, when they ran out of things to talk about.

Their venue for Chinese checkers and love-making was the leather couch at the back of the boathouse; they often talked about him sneaking into her bedroom. Going through the house would be impossible – who wasn't afraid of Mrs. Sugarman? – but he could get in through Liz's window if he could pry off the bug screen and lift the sash window from the outside.

When he was in the company of Sandra's clique, he sometimes thought he could do better than Liz Kowtun, maybe because there was so much choice. All the girls in Sandra's clique were tempting, especially when they were all together and showing off their amusement at everything and displaying how close they were to each other. In particular, he found the appeal of Phyllis Ross mysterious because it was her family that had moved into their old house River Heights. His mother said that the Rosses had bought it on the cheap by cahooting with the goyim at the bank.

Even more mystifying was that he'd sometimes catch himself staring at Becky Gilman, wondering about kissing her, because it was her father and uncle who had bankrupted Bret's father in the first place. Some evenings, the entire clique would walk down Prospect toward town and the arcade. They walked in clumps or pairs right down the middle of the road forcing traffic to slow down and go around them. One night he noticed the 'For Sale' sign was still on the cottage on First Avenue, which allayed the guilt he'd been feeling for not having phoned the realtor yet.

As they walked, the girls – in their little world – would whisper to each other, pairing off in crucial conferences, or adjusting each other's hair bands, which he found adorable because they did it in synchronization.

But of them all, Sandra Sugarman was by far the most delectable, in spite of how mentally absent she came off at times, just staring off into space. Sometimes she was physically absent: back in the city, doing her thing, staying home reading, someone would say. His heart sunk. Although he was discrete when asking where she was, whether she was joining them later, or why had she gone into the city, he was persistent, because he just had to know. And when someone said she was driving in with her father to the Beach later that night, his heart soared. Despite the pleasure Liz Kowtun gave him at night, Sandra Sugarman was the goal, and for her he would renounce the temptation to seduce any of the other girls.

There was only one incident involving the clique that left a bitter taste in his mouth. They were in the arcade by the pinball machines, watching Danny Shnatz play King of Diamonds: ringing up points, getting replay after replay. Danny'd been on the same dime for two hours and Bret asked how he could chalk up so many free games.

– What? You don't know how?

His question started a thousand cackles that spread to the girls who hadn't even heard him ask it. The first wave of laughter provoked a second and a third. Bret, cheeks hot, kept his composure, keeping both his embarrassment and resentment in check; these kids, he knew, were easily amused at someone's expense. He'd seen it before, and it was bound to be his turn at some time. Best to get it over with. Liz and Sandra were the only ones who didn't laugh. Sandra came up to his side:

– They do something with the tilt mechanism, she explained to him.

It was the only thing she'd said to him so far that summer that wasn't just pleasantry, that actually had an air of intimacy to it.

Someone mentioned building a bonfire on the beach, and the clique began to mobilize, but he would have gladly just lingered next to Sandra. After that, he sometimes caught Sandra looking at him openly. He was not sure if those looks were out of suspicion or yearning. He thought the latter because the easiest thing to get used to is your own good luck.

FOUR

In May, Bret had brokered his own one-off fat deal, for which Max Shanus promised him payment in the third week of July. Normally – always – he was distributing for Max, through his own kids, and he preferred it that way, but an opportunity had come up, and Max was surprised but okay with it. He was impressed by Bret's fast progress in 'import-export'. 'And he's only 20,' Max would say to people at the crowded pot parties he hosted. Bret sped down Highway 8 – the fastest way into the city – one Monday morning to collect from Max. The expectation of fresh money in his pocket made the drive all the more enjoyable.

Max lived in the prestigious 'Gates' neighbourhood of Winnipeg's Armstrong's Point, in a large unkempt house with broken front-walk slabs, tilting, crumbling, cutting a path across a front yard full of weeds. The house had a patchy lawn in the back that sloped down to the Assiniboine River.

Max was standing in the front room, tucking his hair behind his ears, looking out at Bret through the large picture window. The front room had a shabby beige chesterfield and an immaculate long couch upholstered in a waxy red velvet that no one ever sat on. Max liked to tell people it was once owned by Al Capone, but that was BS.

– Fins and tens okay? Max asked. They were sitting across at the big kitchen table, a tackle box with cash plunked down on the Formica table top along with the breakfast dishes, cups and saucers and the coffee percolator with its light still on.

– Sure. Twenties are good too, Bret said.

– I made good money on this thing you set up. How'd you do it?

– Brains and personality, said Bret.

– You're a card.

Flush with cash, the wad in his pants pocket to boost his confidence, Bret flirted with the promise he'd made to his mother: he thought about putting money down on that cottage on First Avenue, for her, or at least phoning the realtor to ask about it.

– Any chance of doing it again? Max asked.

– It was just a one-time thing, Bret said. A fluke. The guy was liquidating. He thought the narcs were on to him. Sorry.

– Don't apologize. I like initiative. *Carpe diem.* You want to smoke up? Touch the stars before lunch? Or you high on the money?

– I'm high on my holidays.

– Real Jew. Last time a guy didn't smoke up with me, he saw some daylight coming through the rye.

Max was on the puny side so this could only be taken as irony. Or maybe not: Max's body did have sinew and energy and ran on a higher octane. Bret had once seen a razor-thin kid Max's size at Sportsmen's Billiards on Main Street drop a big guy and pummel him furiously on the floor. And another time Bret had seen Max get mad at one of the gophers and the power of Max's seething and verbal abuse had shocked him; the gopher, way, way bigger than Max, had flinched and looked away intimidated.

– Take a hit. Come on. It's new stuff. I need an opinion or surely I must die.

– Okay.

To make room for his hash pipe made from a large chrome

faucet, Max backhanded the table's surface a bit too hard, sending cups and saucers to the floor. In an exaggerated Jewish immigrant accent, making fun of the guy who had the Jewish program on the radio on Sunday mornings, Max said:

– I'm crazy. I told you I'm crazy from lazy. *Mit die baba and da zaida and alles dink.* Hold the faucet. Maybe for you north-enders it's a tap.

The faucet had a patch of window screen on the aerator fastened by copper wire wound around and down the spout.

– Hold it like a man, Max said.

On the screen Max placed a big crumb of hash, ignited it, and Bret sucked the fumes through the faucet stem and out the other end. He got a baseball of vapours in his mouth, as if you'd sucked on an exhaust pipe. Then Max took a turn and sucked and blew till his head disappeared in a cloud.

Everything Max touched went wild and he was always part of everything. He was loud at parties, naturally eager about girls, grubbing for attention but giving much of it to others; he was overbearing and sentimental. Bret had liked him immediately, or had liked his crazy world of exploding stars and madness, but then Bret was only 16 when they'd met, and Max always flattered him.

– Where's Tracie? Bret asked. Maybe she'll want a toke. We should wait before we do another.

– We don't have to wait for her, Max said. She's upstairs in the tub. She's been soaking in there an hour already. Most women want to get rid of wrinkles but she likes them. And that's the problem with *shiksas;* at 35 they're wrinkled; Jewish women are not. They take naps.

Max Shanas had a young steady Bret's age, Tracie Douglass.

Tracie had been Bret's girlfriend for a hot week, but she and her circumstances distressed him: he once went over to her house in Elmwood and, when he knocked, her father threw empties at the door.

He'd met Tracie at a pot party. She was lightweight and sharp, with shiny cheeks and blue eyes. While he stared into her eyes she told him stories about the boys she'd dumped and those she'd dated and antics galore. She quickly bored him but she had an appeal he couldn't slake with just that first night. Six nights followed the first one until he felt nothing was left of it and his feelings for her and her circumstances had eroded.

So he introduced her to Max and Max started dating her, 'for her brains' he said. Seeing Max squire her here and there or smooch and give her hickies at parties rekindled the original feelings Bret'd had for her. Tracie often smiled at Bret. He smiled back and they played the 'eye game', as she called it, for a long time.

There was this one time, however: he had gone over to Max's and went in the back door without knocking, which wasn't unusual because Max never locked his house since he never stashed anything big there. The sound effects of lovemaking coming from the front room were grotesque and obliterated the creaking of the oak floors as Bret tread them.

Tracie was sitting not on the chesterfield but on Max's long couch red velvet couch. Her knees were raised to her shoulders, spread apart, while Max, knees dug into the broadloom, his body between her legs, was unaware that Bret was in the hall behind him looking in. Tracie saw Bret over Max's shoulder and they did their eye game, she bobbing left and right of Max's head, Bret gesturing with a sideways nod that he would leave, then she shaking her head 'no, no.' He watched her eyes as Max continued. She was enjoying herself more with Bret watching, he thought, and he indulged her, and before Max turned around, probably feeling the presence of a ghost, Bret had left. Lately, Bret had noticed that Tracie shuddered whenever Max touched or kissed her. How Max didn't see it, Bret never knew. Max had pulled her up a notch, socially, and she was grateful. But what a price to pay!

Bret finally relented and smoked up again with Max without waiting for Tracie. When the hash nibble on the mesh turned to cinders, he went into Max's bathroom on the main floor, took his time, fondled Max's razor, and fondled his towelling bathrobe, rummaged through the medicine cabinet checking out Max's pill bottles. It had to have been really good hash because Bret thought it had just taken him half an hour to wash his face, and he couldn't feel if the water was warm or hot.

When he came back to the kitchen, Tracie, her wet hair combed straight back in thick grooves, was sitting in the chair Max had sat in, her knees up to cradle her chin, her pink heels on the seat, toes hanging over the edge wiggling.

– Max? he asked her.

– He's gone to Headingly Penitentiary. He's got a client there. A cop who killed an Indian in front of the Occidental Hotel. Kicked him in the head.

– By accident? Bret said, to be funny.

– For fun if you ask me. Terrible mistake, she said. I wouldn't do what Max does.

– Defend cops?

– Be a dealer and defend cops. Seems like pushing your luck. He gets a kick out of it.

She looked sad and in the mood to talk. She put on more lipstick, and he could smell it.

– Do you ever want to leave him? he asked, checking what was left in the coffee percolator.

– No. Not really. A fantasy is not the same as thinking hard about it, is it? Besides, he's nice to me.

There was no eye game because no one else was there, but she was in the mood, Bret thought.

– I'm on the pill now, she said.

They made love for hours in the sunroom at the back of the house on the second floor, which looked down on the Assiniboine River. Tracie had fitted the bed with white sheets so tight it was the best of highs just to slip between them. A bright sun came in through the window and slowly roasted the room. There was a moment when it got too hot for sex and another when the sex was comical because it got mechanical, but it all went off, not without joy, just a smattering of embarrassment. Afterward, they soaped each other in the shower and rinsed off while kissing shoulders. The hollow sucking sounds of kissing in the recesses of collarbones was pleasurable.

They settled in the living room to listen to Joni Mitchell's 'The Circle Game' and 'Both Sides Now' over and over, and then they played Chinese checkers, which Tracie had taught him months before. Max came home soon, around 7 o'clock; it seemed he didn't notice a thing, not even the fact that they both had wet hair.

– You guys hot in here? I'm thinking of getting air-conditioning.

– We're okay, Tracie said, as if she and Bret were the couple.

Bret and Max talked business in the kitchen: Max had some ideas he was monkeying with but didn't elaborate, one in particular was beyond brilliant and top secret, he said. Bret sensed Max might have been worried that Bret would steal it, but he was wrong. They also talked about preparing for the start of university, maybe finding another kid to work with Rob McMaster, Bret's best boy, who had gotten hired as a lineman's assistant for Manitoba Hydro for the summer, and maybe find more kids for Max's three other dealers working at Bret's level. They estimated how much material they'd need ideally for all those university kids wanting to get off.

Then the three of them all went out into a muggy Winnipeg twilight and drove in Bret's car to the Sals for nips. After that, Bret dropped them off and while still in the city thought about taking Highway 9 back to the Beach, which meant he'd drive close to his mother's.

He screwed the knob to tune his transistor radio to an FM R&B program, and while listening to Dionne Warwick sing 'Walk On By' he thought about stopping off at his mom's on Stella Avenue, in spite of the late hour, to give her some of the money, a bonus to what he usually left her in the cookie jar in the kitchen. He was sure she could use it and sure his generosity would make him deserving of good fortune. The feeling of generosity itself was life-affirming and an omen of good things to come. Every time he made a big score, he always thought about giving a bonus to his mother. But tonight, comfortable in the car and with its speed, he felt overwhelmed by a selfish lethargy.

He drove straight past his mother's street and once out on Highway 9, prudent until passing the police trap before Lower Fort Gary, he stretched his gas pedal leg to adjust the wad of cash in the pocket of his cut-offs, and opened up the engine to 90 mph, passing everybody, even coming so close to an oncoming car that his car, the oncoming car, and the car he was passing, were forced to share two lanes. Heart pounding, he pulled off the highway at Lockport for a hotdog and then smoked up. The night was sultry under thick clouds and low thunder; he could hear the barrage of the river shooting the sluices in the dark.

Even before his headlights swept across the municipal signage saying Winnipeg Beach, and after rolling down the window as he slowed up, he could smell his destination: the damp vegetation and the hot tar stuck to sand and cooling gravel. He could see the dense vegetation growing out of the ditches, bulrushes standing stiffly, and past them to the poplars shimmering in stunted woods, and a zillion fishflies thickening the air around the street lamps. He tried to conjure up Liz Kowtun's face, but it was undefined, and other faces appeared.

In the mood for love, he drove to Sandra's cottage and idled the engine maybe 40 feet from the carport, headlights on. Usually immaculately white, the wall of the wing with the bedrooms was now thick and matted black with fishflies.

He killed the engine and in the dark walked to Liz Kowtun's bedroom window, from which he removed the screen screws with a quarter. The inside sash window had already been hoisted up to the jamb to give the breeze a chance to get in. He slid inside head first, pulling his legs in after him. The room was saturated with heat.

In a jiffy Liz Kowtun was standing against him. Her face was the only thing that shone, and it was almost a pure self that he saw. Eyelids shut, Liz put her arms around him and yawned luxuriously. She smelled of deep sleep when they kissed. Flushed, she climbed up his body, her legs getting as far as his waist. A puff of air came into the room and for a second the mugginess vanished.

– You smell nice, she said. – You can come inside me tonight. I got a diaphragm.

– You were in town?

– This morning. Sandra and me. We both got one.

– To share?

– That's funny. I told her I loved you.

– Why?

– Because you're a lovely person.

– Why did you tell her, I mean?

– I've told my friends in Toronto. Why not her? She enjoyed listening.

– About what we do?

– We did Toronto telepathy, and you were the thought I kept sending her. She got it right away. I told her everything. It made her jealous I bet. She didn't think it was indecent. She says I adore you. I'm way gone, she said. Was I too easy maybe?

– For Winnipeg or Toronto?

– You're lovely.

Bret tried to be quiet because he didn't want to wake Mrs. Sugarman; he prided himself on his control of every risk, a skill picked up from dealing. But Liz Kowtun was ravenous that night, stoked by her confession that she had told Sandra everything, as if what they'd done together just became real. Her passion was like nothing he'd experienced, and he was deluding himself with every stroke that no one could hear her. It would have been another beautiful night of lovemaking if Mrs. Sugarman hadn't hit the light switch, exposing their bodies and the window with the screen off. Mrs. Sugarman even took a step inside and looked in each corner as if she expected to see more bodies.

– Get out!

Sandra's mother had a smoker's screech, and it brought Sandra to the door to witness an event that should have been very private for Bret and Liz. He was sure the scream was meant for him, but he worried that it was also meant for Liz.

No longer numb from shock, Bret pulled on his cut-offs without buckling his belt, left his shirt unbuttoned, and with his Keds in one hand he stretched one long leg out the window, puncturing the window screen below, and stepped into thick damp grass up to his ankle. He pulled and shook his bare foot out of the mesh and ran over a greasy carpet of fishflies on the lawn. His long legs wobbled across the gravel drive, and his parked car seemed to recede father into the night the closer he approached it, much like his prospects for a successful marriage to Toronto money.

FIVE

A week later Bret was walking south along the lakeshore, closing in on the Point. The morning had been sunny and dry, the lake flat, but around eleven, the day had started getting clammy and the lake choppy. Clouds on the horizon would probably push in but for the time being it kept getting hotter and hotter.

He spotted Sandra by the water tower. She was on a large white flannel blanket, tanning in a black bikini, and reading *The Magus*. He could smell her suntan lotion from the shore. At first, her body was slightly folded at the hips, an elbow dug into the blanket, her cheek propped up by her fist. Then she shifted and lay first on her front, and then on her back. Orange rinds lay by one naked thigh.

He noticed for the first time that she had beautiful feet and wondered why he hadn't noticed that before, given that she was always barefoot or in thongs. Actually, he hadn't inventoried her at all, not part by part. Nothing real had yet to break through his idea of her.

He felt embarrassed to be watching her, but he was also curious to find out what had happened to Liz Kowtun. During the week, he had been puzzled about the bitterness he felt for no longer having Liz to be adored by and to play at being in love with, even though venal intent had dulled the sensation of being in love from the start.

To make things worse, since that night, he was no longer part of Sandra's clique. He had been spent a lot of time during the week wondering what he had done to deserve his punishment, what promise he had broken or hadn't made good on yet. Like a tongue that searches out the sore tooth, he thought about not having phoned the realtor about that cottage for sale.

Friendless, he had spent most of the week riding his bike up and down Prospect, re-visiting places in search of feeling, looking out at the lake, smelling the hot tar sticking to the bike treads and spokes, avoiding Sandra's clique and their hangouts. Every time he pedalled past the cottage for sale on First he hoped it would be sold, a *fait accompli* that would excuse him of his guilt. But the 'For Sale' sign was still up, albeit tilting a bit to the left.

One day he stopped at McGregor's Drugstore to make phone calls to his own gophers, especially Rob McMaster, and then Tim Drummond. He also called Max who told him he was going to Morocco soon on business although giving no details about his trip. Max wasn't much in a mood to talk, so Bret asked him to put Tracie on the line, and her voice served as a port in a storm for his emptiness. If his loneliness didn't abate, he had a plan to visit Tracie once Max had left for Morocco. He wanted to do that Toronto telepathy thing with her.

He slept erratically on the veranda at night and looked at himself in the round mirror a lot during the day: combing his hair, grooming himself. He had often been told that he was handsome – a million times by Liz Kowtun – but had never believed it.

Some mornings he drove to the government pier in Gimli to watch the men and boys fishing for pickerel off the government pier; in the afternoons he went to Sandy Hook and had a hamburger, a slice of Boston cream pie and a Coke float.

Some evenings he did what people do when they have nothing to do: he went to the movies. The Winnipeg Beach Theatre had closed when the Boardwalk closed but the Gimli Theatre was thriving and re-ran feature films people had seen or missed in the city during the winter. They showed two films per night and changed the films every two days. He'd seen some strange and disturbing movies there that he normally wouldn't have. Before bed, to get himself to calm down, he'd take a strenuous bike ride in the dark to the Point and back, or sometimes swim a couple of miles in the lake just to feel tired, to feel something.

Now, he was hesitant to approach Sandra on her beach blanket while she was enjoying her book: she had seen him naked. He was also still nettled at Sandra's mother for spoiling things with Liz Kowtun, and he felt insulted for Liz, for her having been seen naked too. It was a repetitive cutting memory, and, mixed with loneliness and boredom, it made him think about packing up and going back to the city; sleeping in his own bed at his mother's, talking to Carl, and cheating on Max with Tracie.

But Sandra, shifting position once again on her blanket, changed things: he loped, then walked with 'cool' from the shore to the edge of Sandra's blanket. She shielded her eyes from the sun to look up at him hovering over her, casting an intense shadow. She slid her sunglasses half-way down her nose.

– My mother sent Liz back to Toronto, Sandra said. She said she didn't like Liz having a 'sexual liaison' under her roof. That's the expression she used. Sent her back the next day, you know. It was a hundred degrees in Winnipeg. She just dumped her at the airport. Didn't go in with her. She had a golf game that morning and missed it. With Mrs. Pearlman, who already thinks my mother golfs too slowly. She hates you.

– I figured that.

– Doesn't want to see you around the cottage.

– Then you'll have to visit me at mine.

– Maybe, she said.

– What kind of maybe is that?

– A categorical maybe.

– Why?

– Where is your cottage? she asked.

– On Ash. Number 18. *Winners* it says.

– For the Winograds? More like 'losers' now. They don't come to the Beach anymore. Deaths in the family. My mother has a million friends on Ash.

– You can come through the back lane.

– Right. Yeah.

– The back door's always unlocked.

– Did I kiss you once? she asked.

Bret had never brought up that day to Sandra, even though he'd had chances. It had nagged him that he hadn't. A lone black cloud passed over them now, and she stopped shielding her eyes. A limp hand came to rest on her thigh. He felt at a great disadvantage because there was no happy memory in his life that he had recalled more often than that kiss.

– Eight years ago, he finally said.   – On your old dock. It lasted twenty minutes.

– Did you time it?

– With a stopwatch in my pocket.

– That's what was in your pocket.

Bret couldn't believe the intense burn of his blush.

– Could you get me some chips from Dorothy's? I can't go with you. My mother would have a conniption if she found out

I was getting chips with you. She doesn't want to see you in town either. She says you should pay for the screen. He didn't even offer, she keeps saying. Tons and tons of vinegar, please.

Bret walked under the water tower and crossed the sunny lot of rubble where the old wood roller coaster used to be. The air was hotter, muggier, the weeds were pungent. He felt faint. He wished the storm clouds would come already. Luckily, there was an awning over the chips window and no line-up, and French fries were already spitting in the chipper.

He walked back to Sandra with her chips. The bottom of the paper bag had greased up fast and was ready to tear so he had to hold it from the bottom and when one palm burned he passed it to the other.

– Not enough vinegar, she said, chewing on two chips, sucking in air to cool them.

– Sorry. But I put in tons.

– Tons and tons, was what I said.

This first impediment to pleasing her pleased him. The fact that she liked much more vinegar than tons of vinegar was a piece of information he kept safe in his heart. He sat down on the blanket beside her and watched her eat her hot soggy chips. The bottom of the paper bag had disintegrated and her white beach blanket was stained with grease.

– Whose boat is that?

– Where?

Bret stole a chip when she turned to look, and she slapped his hand, harder than in a joke. He stole another one with his other hand and gobbled them both.

– My chips!

– Just one more.

He stole a third chip and she slapped his hand again, but it was just a love tap this time.

– There's a letter for you from Liz. It came special delivery to the city, to my dad's office. She must've written it as soon as she got off the plane. Maybe on it. Another one came yesterday. Addressed to my dad's office, too. She's petrified to mail it here. Dad brought them. Wednesdays the husbands drive in. For you know what. Do you want to see them?

– Sure. Bring them over. Like I said before. Back door's always unlocked.

– You know Liz Kowtun's family's been struggling.

– Are they wrestlers? he joked.

– You know what I mean. Her father lost the business a few years ago.

– I thought she was rich.

– Nah. They were once. Toronto rich.

Bret didn't know if what she was telling him was good news or bad. He had been disappointed for nothing. Mind you, he liked Liz now more than before.

– What about the cashmere sweaters? he asked. And that charm bracelet?

– My stuff.

– Her sandals looked expensive.

– Rich kids go barefoot or wear thongs. Haven't you been paying attention?

She was right. All the kids in Sandra's clique had their soles stained with specks of tar and they had dust on their toes the same colour as the cement floor of the arcade where they hung out, playing pinball, with an endless supply of dimes. They almost always got replays and sometimes played for hours on a single dime, exasperating the arcade manager. Wasn't fair, Bret thought.

– Did you fall in love with Liz? She was crazy about you. Thought you were gorgeous.

– She told you that?

– Every day. She got me to play Toronto telepathy so she could talk about you.

Bret put on a good guy act, for whom love is a big deal, easy because it was a big deal for him.

– She was lovely.

– Should I come over tonight and bring the letters? Sandra said.

– I'll be home. Do you play Chinese checkers?

– Would you watch my blanket? I'm going to have a swim and pee.

– I'll go in too.

– Then who'll watch my blanket?

He realized then that she was pulling his leg. He'd have to remember to stay more alert.

She ran in and when the water reached her hips she dove into a wave and came up smiling; it gave him satisfaction to see her smile directly at him, so he stopped watching her blanket and ran in. The lake was known for its sudden treachery, and had got choppy fast. The waves shoved and pulled their bodies to and fro, but all at once the first thunderclap sounded and it started to rain big drops.

– We'll get electrocuted, she shouted.

Just then, a strong wave smacked against him and he was shoved in her direction. She pushed him away like he had encroached on her on purpose and ran out of the lake. He waded slowly back to shore, big drops puncturing the sand.

He stood there, rained on, looking at nothing, while she put on her shift and slid the little rubber post of her thongs between her big toe and second toe and gathered up her blanket and books.

– Come over to my place, he said.

– I have to go. I hate driving in the rain.

– I'll drive you.

– Nah. I'll come over later.

– When?

– I don't know.

– What if I'm not home?

– I'll go in and wait.

– How?

– You always leave the back door unlocked, you said.

– I'm going home now. I'll get soaked.

He was hoping she'd offer him a ride, but she had to be scared her mother's friends would see them.

– I'll meet you at your house. Now's a good time, she said and dashed to her mother's Thunderbird parked in the lot.

The storm lasted less than half an hour, and he waited for her at his cottage, having showered and spruced up with care. Tuning his transistor radio to a Top 40 station, he reclined patiently on the daybed in the back veranda and continued waiting.

When the storm was over, the sun came out and his backyard became steamy and filled with mosquitoes. The blackbirds began singing.

By evening the sun was a red ball that filled his back door. He stared out the screen daydreaming, expecting she would saunter down the lane, up his back steps and into the veranda and be in his arms any minute. When he realized she wasn't coming it was past twilight, and the blackbirds had stopped singing.

SIX

Two days later, in the early evening, he was standing alone on baked pavement in line in front of the Gimli Theatre. The sun was still hot; the sky blue. Icelandic girls were conversing quietly just ahead of him, their hair white and full of sheen. He bought a ticket for the double feature: *Bullitt* and *No Way to Treat a Lady*.

The *Bullitt* poster had appealed to him: Steve McQueen standing alone, wearing a black turtleneck and shoulder holster. He looked important and expectant, concerned with himself. McQueen's hair was the same colour as his, and it happened to be cut the same way. Same sideburns.

Inside the air-conditioned cinema, he bought a box of popcorn, and a pack of Thrills, and let the usher find him an aisle seat eight rows behind Sandra and her parents. He couldn't believe his luck that she was there, and he felt his heart thwack his rib cage.

He watched Sandra in profile whispering to her mother. The theatre went dark and a Pink Panther cartoon flashed on the screen, the soundtrack came on, garbled at first, then clear and soothing. The entire audience sighed with delight at the opening chords of the Pink Panther song. Sandra twisted her head around and saw him. He cocked his chin upward and she did the same to him, adding a guilty smile to say 'sorry about the other day, sorry you waited for nothing', he thought. She whispered something to her mother and was suddenly walking up the sloping aisle towards him, carrying her copy of *The Magus*. How fortunate would he be if she stopped to wave, or touched his shoulder, or sat beside him!

She did all three, and their whispering began, his head turning to her ear, then her head turning to his. Bret was wary that Mrs. Sugarman might turn around and see their faces so close together.

– Why you carrying that book around? he asked.

– Can't put it down.

– You didn't come over the other day. I waited for you.

– Like a girl waits?

– Like a boy.

– My parents had company. The Walshes. Minnow and Lenore? They just came back from Japan. They bought a new convertible Lincoln Continental. You could kill Kennedy in it. We had to see it. And their 400 slides of Mount Fuji. You still want those letters from Liz?

– How about tonight?

– I have to get back to my seat. I told them I was going for popcorn.

– Take mine.

– Has it got butter?

– No.

– I also told them I had to pee.

– Can't help you there.

– We're going for supper after the movie, she said. The Falcon. Meeting the Walshes. So I can't get you her letters tonight.

– I'll drop by your cottage later, he said.

– Right. I suppose you'll take off the screen and step on it again. Believe me, she's going to ask you for money for that screen. And you let the mosquitoes in too that night. She gets welts. We almost had to drive her to Gimli Hospital.

– Which is your room?

– Beside Liz's.

– Right side or left?

– Right. Looking in from the outside. Left is my mother's room. My father has his own room.

– That's sad.

– Your parents sleep in the same room?

– My father sleeps in the cemetery.

– I didn't know he died, Sandra said.

– Eight years ago.

– Oh, I did. I did know. My dad mentioned it. He knew your dad. Said it wasn't fair what happened to him; that life wasn't fair. I hate his negativity. It's reactionary. Listen. Don't you dare come over! My mother's going golfing early tomorrow morning. We can't wake her.

– I thought you said she was lousy at golf.

– She's driving them to the range. Once there, who knows what you call whatever it is she does with them?

– So left of Liz's room?

– No! On the right. Looking in from outside. But don't come in.

'On the right': he stored that information in his heart, next to how she liked tons and tons of vinegar on her chips and butter on her popcorn.

– What's it about? The book?

– It takes place in Greece. On an island. I can't sum up the plot. I read it last summer too. You know, you have the same hair as Steve McQueen. Same burns.

– Have you seen *Bullitt* already?

– When it came out. At the Gaiety. Steve McQueen's boss turns out to be corrupt. He's the bad guy but Steve doesn't know. The plot is ludicrous. And it's supposed to be a progressive movie because he has a live-in girlfriend: Jacqueline Bisset.

Bret had never heard that expression before: progressive movie. He had never thought of movies as being progressive or not: they were never anything other than movies. It would be nice to be articulate like Sandra, express what to think about things.

– I don't feel like watching it now, he said. – You told me the ending. He couldn't believe he was pouting.

– Sorry for spoiling it, she said. – Are you really coming over tonight? You can pay my mother for the screen.

– Really?

– You're so easy to kid.

– You come to my place, he said. The back door has been unlocked two nights now.

– I thought you said it's always unlocked.

He didn't know what to say; she'd caught him in a contradiction. The cartoon ended, and the theatre went black, then came the fluttering and clicking sound of the first feature film spooling in the second projector.

– I have to get back, she said. It's starting.

– Aren't you going to pee?

– That's your business? Can I?

– Can you what?

– Have your popcorn. Since you're not staying. You're lovely, you know. Liz told me that and she was right. Loveliness of person she called it. She's the writer in the family. Those letters are pages and pages. I'll be over tonight to show you. Maybe.

– Right.

– You have to have some faith in people.

Sandra took his popcorn box and flapped in her thongs down the aisle to sit with her parents. As he watched her sway in the dark he thought he'd die. Bret left the theatre and stood outside in the twilit evening, feeling the heat coming down from the marquee bulbs. He watched the pink and blue sky to the west, enjoying the sultry air and the fluttering of a million insects swirling in sudden starbursts around the street lamps that had just gone on.

At home, he put on his transistor radio and had a good scrub with rainwater from the zinc tub, but instead of getting into pyjamas and laying down on the day bed in the veranda to listen to the lake, he took the tissue off a laundered white short-sleeved shirt and got dressed again. He combed his wet hair, then pulled a Coke out of the fridge and a tray of ice from the freezer and sat at the kitchen table. He poured the Coke into a real Coca-Cola glass and plopped in three ice cubes. He didn't know what to do with himself. He didn't even know what mood he was in.

He calculated the time: Sandra would be at least an hour more at the movies (they'd only stay for *Bullitt*); then maybe an hour and a half at The Falcon with the Walshes. Around midnight, he opened the screen door of the back veranda and stepped outside onto the crabgrass, still holding his Coke. He thought that by going outside he could conjure up her presence but only realized she wasn't coming.

He tried to decide if he was still in love with her after all these years, or if he was falling in love with her now. He persuaded himself that his heart was open to both ideas. Then thought not. This lonely exercise, repeated *ad infinitum*, consumed the hours.

Insects hummed and buzzed in and out of his confusion. He was curious to see where he would go after he set his drink down on the hood of his car. He thought about biking it downtown to the arcades to kill time, maybe play bingo, then maybe wait a half hour more to make sure the Sugarmans would be in bed when he surprised Sandra in her bedroom. Or maybe he'd get some chips at Dorothy's and come home and sulk. He decided to go to town. He did an hour's wait at the arcade, then visited the bingo joint, played eight cards and lost, and walked to Dorothy's, which had closed. He began biking north on Prospect, pedalling like mad until he reached the Sugarmans', where he turned off his bike lamp and thought about rousting Sandra.

Only the family cars were in the carport and not a single light was on in the cottage, signs that the Walshes hadn't come back for cake and coffee, and that the family were all asleep. He leaned his bike against a tree and took a quarter out of his pocket. He held it tight in his fist until he was outside Sandra's bedroom, the one to the right of Liz's. He shoved against Sandra's window screen and used the quarter on the screws and then his fingernails to pop her screen out. It bounced silently on the grass, and he leaned it against the wood cladding just in case. In a jiffy, he was head first inside the hot room.

He felt, smelt, and heard Sandra stir under her top sheet. His head burned like his body was the cigarette.

– Shhh, she said.

It was a miracle that she said that and not 'go away'.

– I can't see a thing, he said out loud.

– Don't you know how to whisper?

– I do, he whispered.

– That's better. Shut the window. The mosquitoes!

He lowered the sticky sash window down through its slots as carefully as he could.

– Liz's letters are on the vanity, but I can't show them to you now.

– How come?

– I can't turn on the light. I'm under strict Sugarman surveillance. My mother saw me talking to you at the movies. She's proud of her intuitions.

– Did you open them?

– Did you really come here for the letters?

Liz Kowtun had vanished from his mind and heart, and having gotten this far, he felt self-confident and generous.

– I wanted to know how she was doing. She's the warmest girl I've met.

Sandra stifled a fake snort.

– For Toronto, he added, to be clever, sounding phoney even to himself.

– It must be a hundred degrees in here, he said. How can you sleep?

– I was just finally falling asleep. There was a breeze through the screen. Did you step on it?

– I couldn't wait any longer for you to come over, he said.

He thought that made Sandra think for a moment.

– I didn't say I would for sure.

– You told me 'have faith in people.' And you said 'maybe'. You once told me 'maybe' meant 'yes.'

– When did I tell you that?

– When you let me kiss you eight years ago.

– Come sit on the bed. You'll make less noise. Come. Sit.

– I can hardly see it.

He took a step closer in the dark until he felt the sheet against his knees. She picked up *The Magus*, which had slipped from her hand onto her lap while drifting off to sleep, and placed it on the night table. Hoisted on an elbow, she looked up at him. His love caught fire.

– You really can't put it down, he said. What's it about?

– Perception. It takes place on Phraxos, an island in Greece.

– Perception.

– Sit, she said. – And whisper.

Feeling truly invited, he sat on the edge of the bed, in the triangle where her body bent, tucked into her belly but not facing her. He had to twist his trunk to look down at her face and make out her eyes.

– You are gorgeous, she said out loud.

– What happened to whispering? Isn't your mother next door?

– It's Wednesday night. She's sleeping in my father's room. Are you hungry?

– No.

– Can you get me some cheesecake from the fridge?

– It'll wake them up.

– It's Wednesday. They won't hear you. My father goes out like a light after it.

– What about your mother?

– She watches TV.

Bret tiptoed to the fridge. He'd never seen one with two doors or loaded with so many goodies. He rummaged and found the piece of cheesecake with a toothpick holding up the saran wrap. He brought it back to her room and watched her eat it with her fingers, which was more intimate than anything sexual he could think of.

He stayed until dawn. Before leaving he scooped up Liz Kowtun's letters from off the vanity. Sandra didn't want them in her sight, she had said. After stepping through the window into the dew, he replaced the screen and tightened the screws with his quarter.

SEVEN

He slept till noon in his back veranda and woke in a patch of hot sun, fingering the little pad of sweat below his Adam's apple. There was nothing in his fridge so he biked it to the marina to get a cold Coke at the bait and gas shop. He took a gulp and the Coke tickled his nose. The sun was beating straight down and it was hard to look directly into the flat water between the boats. He sat on the dock in a lawn chair and sipped his drink slowly while a local girl who pumped the gas and worked the cash register was sweeping up around him.

A polished wooden inboard nosed into a slot between two lustreless fibreglass outboards. It looked a lot like the boat in the Sugarmans' boathouse, but more luminous and luxurious in the sunlight. Bret saw a canvas shoe grip the dock boards. Then he heard a voice:

– Bret Yeatman?

– Marty?

Bret hadn't seen Marty Saunders for a couple of years, back when Bret was still pushing direct. Marty had been a good customer; actually, more than a customer. The son of a garment tycoon, Marty was a pot connoisseur, and being a few years older than Bret, he had real money, not just an allowance, because he had dropped out of university from boredom, not failure, and had gone into his father's business, expanding it. Smugger than Bret remembered him, Marty recapped his last few years as a prince.

– I must have 150 people under me now, Marty said.

– Hard on the elbows, Bret said.

Marty's cackle was annoying, but Bret was pleased with himself for making him laugh.

– Sore elbows? I get by, when I get high, said Marty.

Bret had never met anyone as keen for talking about weed, or any drugs, for that matter. Marty's family thought they deserved better than Winnipeg Beach and had built a winterized cottage so far east of the city that it was in Ontario. Tucked safely away from what they considered the 'grosser' Jews, their cottage was on a small island where people took their boating and cocktails seriously. Marty also liked being close to a B'nai Brith Camp, so he could pick up 15-year-olds, a habit he couldn't kick even at 23. Marty and Bret had been pretty close at one time – not that Marty had ever invited Bret out to his cottage – but Bret had spent many a night with him and had even crashed in Marty's rec room in the city when they'd been zonked. They were close only the way potheads can be before realizing they aren't friends: just acquaintances and best keep it that way.

– I thought you hated Winnipeg Beach? Bret asked.

– Long story.

– The short story?

– Call it slumming.

– I will.

– You should.

– Where are you staying?

– With my aunt and uncle.

– Where?

– Lakefront. Natch.

– Natch.

– With the Sugarmans, Marty said. – This is their boat. I came to gas it up.

Bret checked the boat again, and recognized it. Things started adding up.

– Sandra Sugarman your relative?

– First cousin, said Marty, holding back a snigger. She's choice, huh?

– Sure.

– Don't tell anybody, but I jumped her once in *her* car *while* she was going steady with Stevie Bilinkoff. The night of the day she got her driver's licence. We were celebrating.

Some way to celebrate, Bret thought.

Marty twisted his lips into a cruel smile as if he knew how Bret felt about Sandra.

– Some BS: that thing that girls really wanting it, said Marty. – She didn't. Wasn't willing. She kicked hard. Kneed me nuts-wise, but I left more bruises on her. At least she knows how to keep a secret.

– But you don't.

– It's her secret, not mine. Don't tell her you know.

– You mean don't tell her you told me.

– She forgave me, man; I convinced her. And you know why? Because she ran around. Put out. And not just to Stevie Bilinkoff. You should have seen how she dressed then. Like a hooker.

– All teenage girls dress like hookers. Actually, that's where hookers get the dress code.

– You get off with her?

Bret's story about smooching for twenty minutes with Sandra on her pier eight years earlier seemed like a kindergarten tale compared to Ritchie's, and he wasn't going to let on that he had made love to her the night before.

– Fucking Sugarmans, Marty said. – Her father's a douche-bag. Hasn't talked to my father in years. Holds a grudge. Give me a bit of your Coke?

Bret passed the bottle and Marty wiped the rim with his shirt before taking a swig.

– Yeatman's germs. Remember that? Marty swigged and burped.

Then, smiling, because he still didn't know right from wrong, he told Bret anecdotes about the Sugarmans: some real gems. He drank down the rest of Bret's Coke, which he said was warm, as if that was Bret's fault, and threw the bottle in the marina and watched it sink.

– Just a second, Marty said. I've got to gas up.

Marty hopped back into the inboard, backed it out into the channel, gunned forward, making suds, spinning the nose high, then let it slap down before he slid it up beside the gas pump.

He honked hard. The local girl came out and flipped the gas pump lever. Marty popped the gas cap and slid the nozzle in himself before flicking his fingers to shoo the girl away. Bret got up and stood next to him at the pump to watch and said to Bret, his chin pointing at the girl going back into the bait shop.

– Ball her?

– She's only 13.

– If she can unwrap the tampon?

– She's a kid.

– This pump is so fucking slow. It's what I mean about this place.

– It's summer. What's your rush?

– You still selling? Marty asked.

57

— Nothing direct. You still buying?

— Nothing direct, is it? Look at you! You got kids pushing at the Timothy Eaton statue? The only anti-Semite who put a smile on my face soon as I saw him.

— What do you need?

— To get through the weekend in this mosquito-infested shithole *and* the smell of fishflies I'd spend up to fifty bucks. Cash. My mother's trying to patch things up with my aunt, get the brothers to talk to each other. She's into *mitzvahs*. Sandra's father and my father are brothers. It was a business thing they had going together; something happened they split up years back. Someone got fucked. Now they want to put the family together again. I could puke.

— Not here, please.

— Right into the marina. Watch me. Mind you, with this water nobody'd notice. Not Lake of the Woods.

— How come your last name isn't Sugarman? Bret asked. If they're brothers?

— Both brothers were Saunders. Sandra's father changed it to Sugarman.

— Seriously?

— No. I'm BS'ing you. My father changed it to Saunders. Sugarman was too Jewish, my mother said. And now she's into doing *mitzvahs*! And she's become a Hadassah big shot. She was a Rosenthal. Jewish. Not Jewish. Too Jewish. Bring me something. Cheer me up. You want to see the fifty bucks?

— I don't deal direct, Bret said.

— Ever hear of an exception? Why don't you come over? I'm staying at their cottage. I mean we're staying at their cottage. They don't even have air-conditioning.

58

– Can't. Sandra's mother kicked me out for good.

– What for?

– Caught me in bed with their houseguest. Scared me shitless. I went out through the window. She wants me to pay for the screen.

– Busted their screen? Who was the guest?

– Liz Kowtun. Sandra's cousin from Toronto. Your cousin, I guess. They sent her home.

– Not my cousin. The Kowtuns are on my aunt Bella's side. So that's why there's no screen in my room. It's suffocating at night and I can't open the window for the mosquitoes. You went for Liz? She has short legs. She's a *shnorrer*. All the Kowtuns. I thought you'd go for Sandra. Guy like you. And Sandra's a cinch. I have a list of everyone who's balled her.

– Really?

– You're so gullible. I'm joking.

Marty was a natural needler. He enjoyed examining Bret's face after sucking him in. Bret regretted having mentioned Liz because he couldn't lay his cards on the table about Sandra. But now he didn't have to.

– You're after Sandra Sugarman, aren't you? If you went after my Aunt Bella that'd be a hat trick. I could tell you things about Bella Sugarman, too.

The possibilities for malice got Marty excited. Hurting other people was something he was good at: he loved slander and scandal, the joy of either, the fear of them as well. When things went around about him or his family he relished the notoriety. And yet the guy was mellow when he was high, Bret remembered. Even kind. Almost a different person.

– Finally, Marty said, as the gas pump clicked off. – It's these hicks out here.

The girl came out and Marty paid her for the gas, teasing her about the pump, saying he could pump harder. But she looked at him perplexed.

He followed her – mimicking her walk – into the bait store for his change. He came out with a bottle of Coke for himself, offered some to Bret, who waved it off.

– Sandra's a bitch, Marty said. – You should know what you're getting into. She's lost a lot of her Jewish friends. She's not nice to anyone.

– She's nice to me, Bret said, regretting it.

– If you want in with the Sugarmans, I can fix that for you. You fuck Sandra the right way and you could be a Sugarman. You tell a Jewish girl you love them and they do anything. They'll go down on you. But you have to marry them.

– I'll have to pay for the screen I broke.

– You're stupid.

– I'm kidding, said Bret.

Bret thought Marty'd get his joke, but Marty only laughed at his own and had the monopoly on teasing.

– Just get me something, Marty said.

– I don't deal direct

– You keep saying that. Make an exception.

– I never handle anything personally anymore.

– You finger fuck her yet?

– Why are you asking?

– I can fix things with my auntie for you. Maybe fix that screen too.

– How are you going to fix things with Mrs. Sugarman for me?

– You'll see.

– How?

– Bella has the hots. For me. She's choice too. I fingered her once under her bathing suit. Lots of hair. I made her smell my finger. Oh, yeah.

– Come on?

– You are so gullible. Listen. I can get you an invite. She's probably over it. They can buy a million screens. Bella doesn't like her own sister or the Kowtuns or Liz anyway. You probably did her a favour. They won't have to invite her back anymore. The Sugarmans won't even tell anyone the Kowtuns are broke. And that's on her side. My aunt's lucky that her sister lives in Toronto. She wouldn't live them down here. So?

Bret's brain churned the arrangements that would have to be made to get Marty some dope. Stoners were relentless.

– This afternoon at the park where the roller rink used to be, Marty said. – Across from McGregor's Drugs there's a picnic table close to the street. Be there at five. No leaves, no seeds.

– Natch.

Marty threw his Coke bottle into the marina and then he bounced off the pier into the Sugarman's inboard. He started the engine and revved it until the water bubbled and smoked. The noise was loud, rumbling and annoying. The smell of gas burned Bret's nostrils.

– Tomorrow at 11:00. Brunch at the Sugarman's, Marty said, before pushing the accelerator lever hard, making the inboard's nose lift, generating a wake that slopped against the piers.

Bret phoned Rob McMaster from the pay phone in front of McGregor's Drugs.

Rob, compliant by nature – his best boy – drove out that afternoon on his day off with merchandise in a paper bag with enough shit in it to keep Marty high and happy the whole weekend.

At ten to five, Bret was standing in front of the drugstore, scrutinizing the dead drop, his narc radar prickly, eyes on the paper bag Rob had left on the picnic table until Marty, at the agreed time, scooped it up and carried it back to his red Corvette. Bret never touched the bag, just watched it. That was his policy.

Marty and Bret smiled at each other from about fifty yards away. Marty pulled his car up in front of the drugstore and invited Bret for a sail on the Sugarman's sloop the next morning, before the brunch.

– I didn't know they had a sailboat, Bret said.

– It's moored at the marina. A beaut. By the big pier with the big boats. Meet me here at 10. We'll sail it to the Sugarman's dock in time for brunch.

– What about Mrs. Sugarman?

– That's all patched up already. I have dope on her and she knows it.

– Why?

– She's been sleeping with this guy I know. At the Motor Lodge on Pembina Highway. I've got Polaroids the guy gave me.

– Get off it. Really?

– You're so gullible it kills me.

EIGHT

He was roused from bed the next morning by a pressure on his chest that he relieved with three deep breaths. The sun was already softening the tar on the roads, and he could sense from the smell that it was what his mother called 'a beach day' during their holiday eight years earlier: it would be sweltering by 9.

He opened Liz Kowtun's letters. From the first word of the first line of the first letter, Bret knew that Liz Kowtun's heart was in shreds. He felt her misery, but he had little will to do anything about it. It was too late. But he did begin a letter to her: 'Dear Liz, I've been thinking of you so much that writing you seemed unnecessary.'

The lie brought on such lethargy that it made it impossible for him to continue, and he left the pen diagonally on the paper and went to wait for Marty at the marina for the sail ride. Bret wondered when Marty would pay him. 'The richer the kid, the longer they took to pay.' Marty told Bret once that rich kids weren't ashamed about not having cash on them; in short, they didn't *have to* mooch and so when they mooched it wasn't mooching.

The Sugarmans had a long, white ash sloop that was the most stylish of the half dozen yachts moored along the big pier: the other yachts were ugly gin tubs with squat cabins and sliding glass doors. His mother once told him that the Blooms went skinny-dipping off theirs.

It was a fine morning for a sail. The air was still crisp but the sun was high enough to flicker off the chrome trim. Bret could see his Keds in the deck planks, which had been varnished to a glass sheen.

The sail snapped, billowed, and they darted past the pelicans, crossing the bay north to the Point. Marty was a competent sailor and Bret followed his instructions to learn how it was done, feeling defensive and annoyed by Marty's tone.

– Don't let the main out!

– What's the main?

– Don't let it out! You've snagged it. Fuck! Just let me. Fuck a duck! Go sit on the bow and don't move. Watch the boom!

Bret sat on the bow and let his mind melt into the morning light on the lake's surface, which resembled sparks pitched in great handfuls over the surface.

– We're going to dock it in the marina, Marty said.

– I thought we were sailing right to the Sugarmans.

– My car is here. We'll drive. I'd have to take them out for a sail afterwards and I'm pooped. I smoked it all last night. Hit after hit.

Bret was disappointed; he'd imagined he'd be making an entrance sailing up to their dock.

The returning sloop glided smoothly, a couple yards parallel to the large pier, creeping up to its moorings. Marty seemed exhilarated by his performance. He had Bret throw the fenders over just before the boat could crack against the pier struts. Then Bret, as he was told, jumped onto the pier to pick up the bowline Marty tossed at him. There were now a few boaters on the bobbing docks across from the big pier, and Bret didn't want Marty shouting at him like he was a dumbass. He fastened the

64

aft and bow lines to the iron cleats. Marty later corrected Bret's knots smartly.

Bret looked out across the lake to appreciate how far they had sailed. And then suddenly they were crunching fishflies with Marty's tires and parking on the Sugarman carport behind the cottage. As they rounded the corner to the side lawn, Marty dipped his head in confidence.

– Stay cool. It might be raining knives.

– Sounds pretty quiet.

They followed the path along the side lawn.

– Hear that? Marty asked.

– What?

– My mother's voice. Crone drone. She talks a lot now, not like before. Logorrhoea.

They turned the corner onto the big front lawn that sloped down to the lake, walking towards the front deck, to the brunch in progress. Suddenly, Marty slipped something into the right pocket of Bret's cut-offs. Bret knew it was cash and it unsettled him that he'd been paid in such close vicinity to the Sugarman's; it left a taste of shame in his mouth that only a social climber recognizes.

– Honestly, Marty whispered, not noticing Bret's discomfort. – My mother has logorrhoea. It was diagnosed in Rochester. They're considering surgery.

– Really? I don't remember her talking a lot.

– They might do something with the tongue. Stretching it or something.

– Come on. Really?

– You believe everything I say.

As they walked up the steps of the wide deck, Bret heard it: a soft drone coming from Marty's mother, Fanny.

– Don't get me started on renters, Fanny was saying. – I wrote the book.

– Watch out Tolstoy! Marty muttered.

Bret hoped that he wouldn't be interrogated about his cottage.

On the Sugarman's front deck, in the heat of the sun, a spotless calico had been spread over an iron table. Lemon porcelain cups and saucers and breakfast plates had been arranged, with a place setting for Bret. There were tumblers for juice, a matching crystal juice pitcher, a silver coffee pot and silver cream pitcher, a platter of pickled herring, another with halved pink grapefruit sprinkled with sugar, a basket of bagels and a sliced koilage and poppy seed rolls, two silver butter dishes, one with butter, one with cream cheese, a silver chafing dish with bacon and sausages sweating inside, and a platter of fat-marbled corned beef.

– It's like an Israeli cabinet meeting, Marty said. He broke himself up, but he was the only one who laughed.

To avoid not only Mrs. Sugarman's but everybody's eyes, Bret gazed at the lake. There were no introductions so Bret just sat down at the place set for him while Marty sat between his parents, Fanny, and his father Lawrence Saunders, who had a large egg-coloured hearing aid in his ear. Everyone ignored Bret, including Sandra in a black bikini top and jean cut-offs, and his ridiculous idea that they had been expecting him simply vanished.

Sandra was sitting between her parents, reading *The Magus*, dreaming of Phraxos. Her face, which he thought he had memorized, was unfamiliar and closed to any acknowledgement. Had they made love or not in her bedroom the other night?

Mrs. Sugarman, after an initial glimpse, averted her eyes from Bret's and went back to browsing her *Cosmopolitan*, looking up every once in a while at Fanny, her sister-in-law, who had the floor, and tattled on about the difference between cottage owners and cottage renters and between weekly renters and season renters and between Winnipeg Beach renters and Lake of the Woods renters. Mrs. Sugarman purposefully made an intermittent show of paying attention to her.

– But you're talking about renters in Lake of the Woods, Lawrence, her husband said. – You're *farmishing* things.

– It goes for everywhere, Fanny said, buttering a slice of koilage. – There are just more renters in Winnipeg Beach. A renter just doesn't look after the property.

– You can't generalize, said Sandra's father, Ben Sugarman, paying attention to Fanny out of pity, Bret thought.

– You say that because your father voted CCF, Fanny said. He was a Socialist, and now people go on welfare because they can.

Like an itch you know you should never scratch, Bret could not help himself and made eye contact with Mrs. Sugarman, to show charm, and gratitude. Bella Sugarman's eyes were blue and smart; they gave an impression about what she was probably like when she was young. She was wearing a black peignoir with red peonies open over a black bathing suit fronted with a triangle of black gauze from her collarbones to her navel: the ensemble set off by very red lipstick. He began to sketch a vague smile for her that would serve as an apology for Liz Kowtun and breaking the screen.

Her eyes slid back to her *Cosmopolitan* magazine, and Bret thought that at any minute she would shoo him off the deck. But then she raised her eyes over the magazine and squinted at him and Bret detected the merest sigh of tolerance slip from her lips.

Sandra quickly looked at him, a look that warned him from trying to make further eye contact with her mother.

67

He did though, one last time, and Mrs. Sugarman responded with a genuinely friendly frump; he was grateful and returned it, but that was the end of it. Sandra noticed and put her nose back in her book.

Bret wondered what Marty had done to affect a change in Bella Sugarman's attitude towards him. During his two weeks with Liz Kowtun he had never met Mrs. Sugarman, until that night she caught them, so all he knew of her was that shriek, from which he'd made certain inferences.

He imagined, flattering himself, that Marty had told them he was a business associate, perhaps of some worth or promise, surmising that something like that had impressed her into lenience, made her set a place for him. Or, was it something other than Bret's good luck that had made Mrs. Sugarman come to assume, because of Marty's familiarity with him, that Bret did not come from muck and manure?

Given that Mrs. Sugarman had 'intuitions', Bret wondered if she had intuited by now that Sandra was having a sexual relationship with him, and maybe that's what inspired her clemency. But then, Sandra was dissembling beautifully, feigning distance, unless she had actually grown indifferent to him.

– Who cares about the differences between owners and renters? Ben Sugarman said to Fanny.

– I, for one, don't, said Lawrence, Mr. Sugarman's brother, shutting his wife down, attempting what he thought was a show of mutuality with his hitherto estranged brother.

– But you have the right to your opinion, Fanny, Ben said, into Fanny's bruised lull.

– I should never talk, Fanny said.

– I'm not saying that, Ben said.

For the first time, Bret took true notice of Ben Sugarman: the guy had an infantile but determined face, and a stocky body like his brother. Ben was comfortable being both grumpy and kind, seeming not to show he knew the difference.

Fanny's silence provided everyone time to fork herring or pour coffee or butter their rolls. Then Marty's mother rolled out on her tongue again:

– I drank too much last night.

– You should never drink, Lawrence said.

– This sun, she said. – It's all I needed. And this stink of fishflies.

– We all drank too much, Ben said.

– Where's your sun hat, Fanny? Lawrence said.

– I hope I didn't say anything offensive, Fanny said.

– You will, Marty said.

– The Winemans told people for years that they owned their cottage but in the end the truth came out, Fanny said. – They lost it and had to rent it from the bank to keep up appearances so people wouldn't talk.

– That went well for them, said Sandra into her book.

– Renters! Marty said. – They should be drowned in algae!

– Leave your mother alone with the sarcasm, Lawrence said to Marty. – Lay off!

– They'd have gotten more respect if they'd told people the truth, Fanny said.

– Those sneaky Winemans, Marty said.

– And the Winemans are not the only ones, Fanny said. – I know the treasurer at Glendale and I can tell you about people you don't even know.

Marty had spoken the truth about his mother. Fanny was enraptured by her own tinny droning voice; the flow of words left her no breath for swallowing her food. It was all gossip, Bret thought, and the closer her friends, the crueller the gossip. Sandra sat through it glowering, trying to read while pretending she was listening.

Bret remembered an incident from a couple years back. He and Marty were smoking up in Marty's rec room. Mrs. Saunders had come downstairs and caught them toking. She tried to look shocked but it came across as dazed. Staring feebly at them, she had struck Bret as absent, mousey, and unkempt; she didn't raise any scruple about what they were doing and just pretended to be looking for something. 'She's looking for her own asshole,' Marty had said, giggling.

Marty had a brother, Laurie – named after Fanny's favourite brother, who had died young. Laurie trained to be a great violinist, which is what Fanny wanted. She pushed him as if she had something to prove to people: he shot himself at 17, after an earlier attempt using a rope over the rafters in their three-car garage. Marty joked that Laurie could string a violin but not himself. But one day, when he was as high as a balloon, Marty told Bret: 'It hurt so much I shit myself.' It was soon after Laurie's death that Mrs. Saunders began talking to beat the band.

Bret compared his status with the prosperous people sitting around the table. He felt like one of the bums he used to see at Assiniboine Downs gawking at the $100 pari-mutuel window. But that memory was from long ago when his father could still afford a $100 ticket. Now, sitting there with all these people he didn't know, he felt like one of those racetrack bums. The best he could do was repress a yawn with his hand to project superiority while trying not to offend as the conversation settled on people he didn't know. But that was all wrong, he told himself, feeling phoney. He decided to reverse course; for his own good he would listen carefully, taking in the information, showing gratitude for being there, and respect for everyone, especially to the nut job, Marty's mother. He wanted a new life, didn't he? He made inquisitive jerks of his head to encourage Fanny's interventions.

Sandra, he saw, sipped her coffee and kept her nose in her book, her mind on her sun-steeped Phraxos. With the rim of his coffee cup resting on his lips, he looked at Sandra several times, waiting to catch her looking at him, but he got nothing, not even a wink. Her indifference worried him and made him aware that his yearning for her outweighed his calculations. His feelings for her were not like the ones he could control for Liz Kowtun. These feelings overwhelmed him. He wondered where feelings like those had hidden themselves for so long, why none of the precocious sex he had before had ever flushed them out.

The two Sugarman brothers, Ben and Lawrence, did not exchange a single word with each other again, but there was a sense they shared an alleviated cordiality, which Bret assumed had been patched together by the wives. Something tremendous had happened in the family history way back, Marty had hinted, and Bret was witness to a psychic relief, even as Marty's mother nattered and fussed about other people.

Feeling reasonably accepted, Bret managed to get down half a bagel with butter and helped himself to a second cup of coffee without spilling. He tried to smile at Mrs. Sugarman but she was unable to respond with anything more than a rictus of lenity.

– Sandra? she asked suddenly.

– Present, Sandra snapped sarcastically, alert because she had only been pretending to read.

– My head is aching, Mrs. Sugarman said, pinched and dismal. – So don't start with me. Why don't you give the book a rest and take Marty and Bret out in the canoe?

– What? Are they Indians? said Fanny, who wasn't eager to lose listeners.

– Groan, said Marty, bolting down a roll. – I'm still eating, Auntie Bella.

– It's hot, Sandra answered.

– It's a beach day; and I can't stand watching you reading that book all day again. And your friend looks bored.

– Bella! Let the boy eat something first, Ben said to his wife, nodding at Bret. – He hasn't eaten anything. You're starving him.

– I have, Bret said.

– You had coffee, said Ben Sugarman. – That's not eating.

– He had half a bagel and butter, Sandra said.

– Half a bagel is no bagel, Ben said.

– What does that even mean? Sandra said. – Let him eat how much or how little he wants.

– Look how she's defending him! said Marty's mother, meaning Bret. – Something's going on here. I can tell. I'm psychic. I wasn't even introduced.

– Sandra defends everybody except her own family, said Mrs. Sugarman.

– What's your last name? Fanny asked Bret. She hadn't even asked his first.

– Yeatman, said Mrs. Sugarman, stealing the word from his mouth.

– Morris Yeatman's son? Fanny asked.

– Son and heir, Bret said, which made Sandra's father smile.

– You remember Bret? Marty asked his mother.

– I remember Morris Yeatman from Aberdeen School, Fanny said.

– That's Morris Yeatman's son, Ben said.

– He doesn't look like Morris. Nothing like him.

– Are you sure? Fanny asked Bret.

– He knows who his own father was, Lawrence said. Mind you, you might know better.

– A bit late for introductions, Marty said.

– You should have made them, Mrs. Sugarman said to Marty.

– He's Sandra's friend too, said Marty.

– I knew it, Fanny said. He's more than a friend if you ask me. They're dating. I knew it. I'm psychic.

– You're not psychic, said Lawrence Saunders adjusting his hearing aid, looking terribly unhappily married, but with a bundle.

Bret now gave up the idea that his presence hadn't registered. He had already been discussed and they may have entertained but left unsaid the idea of accepting him, despite what had happened with Liz Kowtun and the window screen. He wondered what Marty had said to Mrs. Sugarman, or what Sandra had said, and whether he was acting the part well enough to match what it was they had said about him.

His prospects had been revived: in a few years he could be spending his summers having brunch in the sun with Sandra and her family on this deck. Perhaps they'd have kids by then. He didn't know what would happen with his mother: whether she would be invited out of courtesy, or whether she would be too intimidated by the Sugarmans to come. For sure, by that time, he'd have bought her her own cottage. He was now in the mood for food, but it was too late. Sandra cracked the spine at the page she was reading and left her book cover side up on the tablecloth.

– Don't lose my place, she said to her mother. Help me with the canoe, she said to Bret, taking his hand and pulling him up. No one objected to her gesture.

– Thank you, Bret said to Mrs. Sugarman.

– You coming or not? Sandra said to Marty.

– Nah.

She and Bret walked down off the deck. She squeezed his hand openly, and he was pleased that no one threw a saucer at the back of his head. Bret stepped inside the boathouse and felt the gorgeous heat floating up to the rafters. Sandra bumped into him after closing the screen door and he took advantage of her proximity to fold her into his arms in total absorption of her body. He had never felt something fit so naturally, nor something quench his yearning for love so conclusively. He had an erection, but he couldn't really feel it because it was irrelevant to his emotion.

– Not here. Not now, she said.

He felt misinterpreted, but attentive to her demands.

– I wasn't …

– Help me take down the canoe.

– Which one?

– The red one. You know you come off being too grateful.

– To who? When?

– To my parents just back there. They don't deserve it.

– They paid for the brunch.

– Just my impression.

– Where are we going?

– You'll see. Somewhere secluded. They can never know we're sleeping together. Not yet.

– Can I still come to your room?

– Just don't step on the screen.

She piloted the canoe deftly, giving him curt instructions as if he were a stranger, and soon she brought the red hull up onto a narrow deserted beach of reeds and stones and sand a few miles up towards Gimli. She tossed out her white flannel blanket first. Head raised to the glaring sun, he surveyed the lake from the shoreline until she pulled down her cut-offs to her ankles and did a light stomp to get her feet out while he shut his eyes tight.

NINE

Two weeks later, he was sleeping in the sun on a chaise-longue on the Sugarman's lawn, next to Sandra, when Sandra's 11-year-old sister arrived.

– She's a mongoloid, Sandra had told him earlier. –They keep her locked up.

– In the attic?

– In a home in Selkirk.

– What's her name?

– Adara.

Bret thought that was the most beautiful girl's name he'd ever heard, and it suited her, sweet and obstinate as she was. Mrs. Sugarman got out of the car last, trying to stand on her dignity in front of Bret, which he supposed had been trampled by the shame of Adara's existence, or the shame of her internment. It was one of the rare times Mrs. Sugarman gave him a genuine smile, spritely and embarrassed. But he felt no empathy for Mrs. Sugarman because it was evident she didn't want it from him.

Adara, who had been institutionalised from birth, loved her family, despite the sparse contact; there were weekly visits to the home in Selkirk, and then Adara spent an entire week with the family every summer at the cottage. Mr. Sugarman was especially fond of her, or made more of a show of it, and took a week's holiday to be with her, the only holiday he took. Adara couldn't speak. Instead of words she uttered grunts of joy on many occasions, especially when someone played with her.

Bret noticed that Mr. Sugarman liked how caring Bret was with Adara. Ben would sometimes stand, his legs spread, feet planted firmly on the grass, fists on his hips, watching her play with Bret in the shallow edge of the lake, or wearing a sun hat and a life vest tucked under her chin in the small rubber dinghy that Bret pushed from behind into deeper waters, kicking with his legs and blowing bubbles to simulate a motor. Adara, hysterical with pleasure, wouldn't let him stop, not until his lips turned purple and she got hungry. Then they munched butter and brown sugar sandwiches underneath two pink Adirondack chairs turned upside down to make a tent.

Although much of his play with Adara was spontaneous, it never escaped his mind that he was also intensifying his relationship with Sandra. Bret imagined Mr. Sugarman was watching him and thinking that if Bret married Sandra he could die peacefully knowing they'd continue to look after Adara. Mr. Sugarman's own father, Sandra had told him, had died at 55 from a massive coronary and, in her words, her father 'enjoyed the neurotic pleasure' of imagining he would too.

On the third day of Adara's visit, the Sugarmans went golfing and Bret and Sandra buckled Adara into her life vest and took her out in the canoe and gave her a toy paddle to use. They landed at the spot that they now called 'their beach', built a driftwood fire and roasted spitted wieners that tasted of sand and ash.

Back at the cottage, in the evening sunshine before supper, Bret let Adara tackle him over and over again on the lawn. This made Mrs. Sugarman smile and nod with what Bret thought was encouragement and affection.

By the fourth day, Adara held Bret's hand whenever she could.

She let him help her with her meals. She shrieked with pleasure when she saw him lean on his knuckles and swing up the lawn, swaying his arms from his shoulders like an ape. All this had to endear him to everyone, he thought. Yet the Sugarmans, despite their smiles and pleasant looks, remained strangers to him, and he felt he was a stranger to them.

His time with Sandra during Adara's stay went unfelt. He remembered one exchange though. They were playing with Adara in the sand, building hills and crowning them with tiny flags.

– My father wants the boathouse cleaned, Sandra said to him. Bret bounced up to his feet.

– I didn't mean right now. I didn't mean you, she laughed. He didn't find it funny.

On the last day of her visit, when she had to let go of Bret's hand to get in Mr. Sugarman's Lincoln Continental for the drive back to the institution in Selkirk, Adara exploded into such a tantrum that she shat herself. Mrs. Sugarman suddenly looked overwhelmed, a weariness of Adara criss-crossing her face, while Mr. Sugarman looked embarrassed. Sandra, grappling with Adara, shouted at Bret to hide behind the boathouse until they left because he was upsetting Adara's departure.

– Get away from her! Don't let her see you!

He felt his cheeks get hot, and he sheltered himself behind the boathouse, mistaking Sandra's terse instructions for criticism. He could still observe the drama, watch Sandra take a deep breath to calm herself down and tug Adara gently back inside to bathe her and help her put a fresh set of clothes. The three Sugarmans, he saw, then steered Adara into the car, and this time – with Bret hiding – Adara was thrilled at the prospect of a car ride. Bret watched the whitewall tires of the Lincoln as they ground gravel until the car disappeared behind a thicket. Then he rode his bike home in a mood.

He didn't go back and unscrew the window screen to get inside Sandra's room that night, to feed on her like the mosquitoes that came in behind him. Instead, he stayed in his veranda and listened to the lake smack the beach, his transistor radio tuned to a jazz program. He smoked and thought about business and not the Sugarmans. His original plan had been not to deal until the summer ended because he already had prospects with Max Shanas for September.

Up until Sandra's rebuke, he had wanted to spend the summer in the sun, relaxing in the heat, engaging as little as possible with the business, enjoying Sandra and his fantasy of integration into her family. But all that seemed ruined now; Sandra had shouted at him in front of her parents, and reliving his humiliation made his cheeks burn as hot now as they had then.

His proud sulking diverted his feelings. He was caught between two punishments for her: never forgiving her, or pressing forward and marrying her for her money. These were foul thoughts that he could only keep at bay by focusing on what he was trying to avoid that summer, which was thinking about business; imagining what Max was up to in Morocco.

He didn't have to wait long. The next morning, Tracie, with a big smile, showed up at his cottage – Max's orders were to pick him up and bring him back into the city. It bothered him that he couldn't refuse, but his pride was also flushed with an excuse for snubbing Sandra for another day.

– I'm not happy you came here, he said.

Tracie lost her smile.

– You don't have a phone. Max said I have to show you something by noon.

Back at Max's house Bret looked at a stack of box sets of Deutsche Gramophon recordings of Beethoven's quartets, which, according to the cancelled postage of the empty box on the table, had come from France.

– So? he asked Tracie.

– Open one.

As soon as he tore the cellophane of one of the flat boxes and peeled it away, he could smell sweat and nutmeg. Instead of records inside, there was a thick disk of compacted hash wrapped in more plastic.

The phone rang. It was Max calling collect from Morocco.

– This was just a test run. Find me an address to send the records to. Go see my realtor!

– Can't Tracie do it?

– She can't rent a house, not even a suite, not even with my guy. If they do a credit check, they'd never rent to her. She's never had a job. And I don't want it in my name.

– I'm not putting it in my name either, said Bret. – You know I don't touch anything wet or dry.

– Put it in Rob's; he has a real job. Just get me an address. It's insane here. Quality. Price. Bulk. Pure kismet, Bret. Not for the greedy. Tangiers-Marseille-Western Canada. Tracie's got the cash. And I left her some voided cheques too for the realtor. She knows where.

– The risk?

– Lustful is the human soul.

– Tracie could have done this with Rob. What did you need me here for?

– I want you to go with her to Rob's. He's your boy. Isn't he always talking about moving out? Getting his own place?

– And kismet? What's that?

– This is long distance.

– What is it?

– Luck or something. Or *bashert*, said Max.

– This is about service, isn't it? Bret said.

– Yeah. You serving me.

Tracie drove him to Rob McMaster's. Rob had the day off. They found him at a tub of cucumbers, helping his mother put up pickles. The three of them visited Max's realtor. That same day Rob, in his name, rented and took occupancy of a furnished bungalow on McMillan Avenue, which Rob was thrilled to move into despite the risk he was running: not only could he now move out of his parents' house, but he was moving up in the organization.

Bret paid the realtor a month's rent with the cash that Tracie gave him. They drove off with Rob standing on the front stoop, waving 'bye,' with a huge grin on his face. Bret promised himself that, if he ever left Max, Rob would have first dibs at taking his slot. Making that promise to himself gave him a positive vibration. He imagined how happy it would make Rob, an image that meshed with his good luck. He didn't understand why he had given Max an argument over the phone. At 5 o'clock, Bret treated Tracie to supper in an air-conditioned steak house, and when she drove them back to Max's it was as sunny and hot as before their meal. They had his radio on and all four windows down but it was still hot in the car. When they got out Bret took his radio inside.

Settled into the beige chesterfield in Max's front room, listening to a Top 40 station from Brandon, he could tell Tracie was in the mood to talk about Max.

– Will you help me? I don't know what to do.

He knew what she meant. – Why don't you leave him?

– Do you still like me?

– Sure.

– You owe me money for taking groceries to your mom's last week.

– Wasn't there money in the jar?

– Not enough.

– How much do I owe you?

– Twenty.

– Okay.

– Do you think it's kismet ... *bashert* ... that Max's away? She asked.

Carrying his radio tucked under her arm, she led him up to the sunroom. It was 8 p.m. but still bright out so she drew the drapes; he thought the sun would never set, the heat would never abate. She found station she liked that was playing 'For What It's Worth.'

– Are you on the pill? Bret asked in the dark, just shoving soft but not thrusting.

– You asked me that the last time.

– Did I?

– Don't worry. The Russians are here.

– Russians?

– The Reds. The Russians. My period. My mom calls it that. You know they took me away from her and dad for two months once. Into foster care. That was scary.

– Should I get a towel?

– I have light ones. And I have to do laundry anyways.

– Are you sleeping in here?

– While Max is away. I like this room.

– It's like an oven.

– Shhh.

He thought the sex with her was better than the last time because he felt his future social status had changed; he made love now feeling self-conscious, as if there were witnesses to the act. Although the other time didn't feel like love either, he had felt their hearts were open and frank. This time it was over quickly, with him feeling ashamed. He got off her and off the bed fast and opened the drapes to the sunset. She sat on the bed, her knees up, toes wiggling behind the big glass ashtray she'd laid on the bed. They both lit up. Her idea. Her shoulders and hair were streaked red by the light that came through the window. He stood at the window, looking at the river and then back at her.

– You've lost weight, he said.

Tracie shivered. Which was a Yes, I have.

– And you've put on a few pounds. Are you eating out a lot?

He thought of the Sugarman's fridge so stocked up you could never find anything.

– Are you lonely without Max? he asked.

– I'm good.

– I don't know why you stay with him.

– That makes two of you, Tracie said.

She laughed at that, a beat before him. Leaning his naked bum against the sill and facing the room, he sighed and looked back across his shoulder at the river and then at her, back and forth. She crushed out her cigarette in the ashtray, and he leaned over and did the same. What was in store for her? he thought, examining her face. She returned the look. He wished he could get hard again right away because of that look, which was frank, instinctive, the look from someone who knows they are doomed.

– Aren't you getting hard again?

– No.

– Why not?

– Can't say.

– Should I drive you back to the Beach?

– I can take the bus tomorrow. You must be sleepy.

– I'm not sleepy, she said.

– Sleep. I'll take the early bus out.

He wanted her to drive him back, but he didn't want her at his cottage again, or near his things, or accidently bumping into Sandra or her friends.

– Come back to bed. Please. It's only nine. Unless you want to go for a walk. I have mosquito lotion.

They made love again. He was not selfish but gentle this time. After that, all he wanted to do was get back to the Beach that night and slip into Sandra's bedroom and patch things up with her. He knew he had overreacted to the incident with Adara and felt sure she would accept his apology. He fell asleep, thinking of Sandra and his apology, without the least concern for Tracie or what she was feeling. At least he felt ashamed of himself for that.

The next morning, when the sun rose at a quarter to six, while Tracie slept, he drew two tens from his wallet and laid them on his pillow to pay his mother's grocery debt. Then he cabbed it to the bus station. He had missed the first bus. While he waited for the second, he scanned the waiting room, which smelled from the sour clothing of the men who had slept the night on the benches. All the weight of his circumstances – Max, Tracie, the business, the Sugarmans, Sandra's rebuke – pressed down on him. For one brief moment, he wished he were as free as the bums sitting on the benches. He was on the cusp of social acceptance, albeit tottering, and that frightened him. To add to his fears, he remembered that promise he had made to buy his mother a cottage at the Beach, a debt that suddenly assumed a galactic scale that could only be repaid by an alliance with the Sugarmans. He made a note to call the realtor of the cottage that was for sale. Then he heard a sweet obstinate voice calling his name.

– Bret! Bret! He turned toward the voice and saw Tracie, but he was slow to react because he couldn't place her there. Reluctantly, his body fit into the arms she had opened up for him. Perplexed, he couldn't fathom her feelings for him, but he felt she comforted him from his fears.

– Do you want me to drive you? Tracie asked. – You left so early.

– I told you 'no'!

– Don't get mad.

– I have my ticket already, he said. – Don't forget to phone Max and tell him Rob's address.

– I won't.

– And my mom's groceries next week?

– Have I ever forgotten?

– No. Why?

– The way you said it.

– I'll make sure there's money in the jar this time. Take a fin for gas.

– Max gave me money for gas before he left.

He watched Tracie hesitate before leaving the depot, standing alone in a rectangle of harsh sunlight in front of the doors, waving, cocking her caring, but used face which he was pretending to ignore. Then she vanished. He knew he didn't want to sleep with her anymore. But he felt grateful for having been close to her. And obligated for her help.

He fell asleep, one temple against the hot bus window, as they passed Lockport. When he opened his eyes, he was back with Sandra on their own little beach, beside her canoe, his heart convulsing, as him and Sandra made love. All of a sudden she asked:

— Can we do it differently? she said.

— How?

She whispered something in his ear.

— I don't know what that means, he said.

— It's not hard I think. According to the literature.

Now they were doing it in a way they had never tried before; her body rucked, her cheek was crushed against her white flannel blanket, her eyes so tightly shut he noticed how short, stiff, and pretty her eyelashes were, and moist from pleasure.

Afterwards, he had a bitter taste in his mouth. He could not bridge the gap between her pleasure and his shame for her, for what she had asked of him. She had turned herself into a stranger just like that. He forced his imagination to harken back to their first kiss on the pier, and he dwelt there to convince himself that innocence still existed for them. It took him several minutes for her strangeness to flip into familiarity and he held on tight to her to retain the nearness. In time, her breathing evened out, his muscles relaxed and he knew her again.

They sat, knees up, facing the lake now. The breeze cooled

their cheeks and kept the mosquitoes away. From the way she hugged her knees, pressing first one cheek to her kneecaps, and then changing to the other cheek, he sensed that she wanted to say something. She did.

– You know, I was in Montreal two years ago.

She didn't elaborate right away, so he kept quiet and let her take her time.

– For an abortion. There's a doctor there. He's even Jewish.

– Did it hurt?

She looked puzzled for a second, as if she had expected him to ask who the father was.

– In my heart. It hurt my heart.

– Were you on the pill?

– I was always forgetting to take it. Some days I'd take two just in case I missed a day.

– Are you forgetting to take it now?

– Don't you want to know who the father was?

– That's a private thing.

– Aren't you feeling jealous?

– I'm feeling bad for you. For your heart. One feeling at a time.

– It was the end of my engagement to Steven Bilinkoff, that's for sure.

– Did *that* hurt?

– Why do you want to know if I was hurt so much?

– Was it because of the abortion?

– Ask him.

– Those are two really bad things, he said. – How did you cope?

– Let's just say that drowning was what kept me afloat.

The rim of the lake pushed up closer to their toes as the waves slopped in, a sign that they would have to leave soon. The breeze was now a series of strong gusts that blew her hair across her nose and cheeks and kept her busy moving it off her face.

– Where were you last night? You didn't come by.

– I was sulking.

– Where?

– In town. I wanted to see my mother. She wasn't feeling well.

– You have lots of people to feel bad for.

– I'd like to buy her a cottage for the summers. I promised her. I think it would get her out of the house more.

– Do you have the money?

– I can get it. I had enough this summer for a down payment. I didn't even look though.

– Too busy with Liz? She's prettier than me. I hate my legs. But then, you were prettier than her.

Sandra had herself a laugh at that.

– Where do you get your money from? she asked.

– Import-export.

He fell back on his elbows now, his chin resting on his chest. He looked out at the enormous lake. Insects swarmed and buzzed between the reeds to protect themselves from the wind. Sandra, on her belly, alongside him, was propped on her elbows, meshing her fingers together under her chin, speaking into the sand and gravel and purple stones.

– Did Becky Gilman's father bankrupt your father? she asked.

– I think that's the story.

– Did he really?

– My father had a door factory up on McPhillips Highway.

– That's what my father said.

His vanity was tickled by knowing that she and her father had had a conversation about him that established a credential of past affluence. He was glad they didn't think he was just a mooch.

– Becky's father and uncle were building an apartment block in East Kildonan and placed an order, Bret said. He and my dad were friends, actually. My dad delivered a thousand doors, but Becky's father didn't pay him. My father ran out of working capital and had to file for bankruptcy.

– A real shit.

– Becky or her father?

– Both of them. It was only business. A long time ago.

– How can you forgive those people?

– It's my father I can't forgive.

Sandra unlocked her fingers and her chin slumped gently into the blanket. He thought about her trip to Montreal. He wondered who had gone with her.

– Were you bitter? she asked.

– Impoverished. You know, your friend Phyllis Ross lives in the house we were evicted from when the bankruptcy trustees liquidated my father's equity.

– How can you stand seeing her?

– Not her fault. He should have protected himself from liability. He screwed up.

Bret was holding back. He stifled the other things he wanted to list as grievances against his father, foremost being his father's self-contempt, which was paraded often at home, and which, in all fairness, came after his gross blunder in business.

– You are prettier than Liz, she said to him, shifting her body to bump it gently against him to underline her joke.

When that wasn't enough for him to react, she rolled him half a turn towards her, pulling his bum until their hipbones knocked. She kissed him for the longest time and when her lips were sore she rolled him off the blanket and onto the sand and then back on again. Then she got into a crouch beside his head.

– My father wants you to visit the factory. He thinks we're getting serious.

After she said this, Sandra lowered her eyes brimming with embarrassment, which he thought was because he had ingratiated himself too fast.

– What for? he said, trying not to show his excitement.

– To see if you like it.

– Tell him thanks.

– You tell him. But you won't like it.

Sandra stood up, brushed sand off the back of her bare thighs and knees and put on her bikini bottom.

– Why wouldn't I like it? he said, looking up.

– It's a *factory*! I don't like it. The workers for sure don't like it. And he thinks he's wasted his life there, so he doesn't like it either. Capital formation is not fun. Waste of time, he calls it. Wasted time. Wasted life. But as he says: 'it is how it is.'

Despite how sinister Sandra presented the factory, for Bret her father's suggestion was another piece of kismet. He was starting to get used to it.

– So you'll go?

– When?

– Next Monday morning. Can you be there?

– I can be there.

– He'll probably take you to lunch. And you'll meet Abe.

– Did you finish your book? he asked.

– Yep.

– What are you going to read now?

– I'm going to read it over again. It's the next best thing to going to Greece. But I'll get there. There are jobs teaching English. Leonard Cohen lived there. I'm coming into some money from my grandfather. In Greece it's always sunny. No mosquitoes. You can live there on five dollars a day.

Bret had a total disregard for what Sandra was suggesting. The invitation to her father's factory outshone Sandra's musings about Greece, outshone the sun even; they were just daydreams anyways, he thought.

– Did it hurt before? he asked.

– Stop with that. Stop apologizing, and stop being grateful.

Scooting out of nowhere, thick black clouds banked inland and a gust flipped her bikini top out of her hands, and she chased it down. A few drops splashed on the thwarts and bow of the canoe. Storm waves built swiftly into a dirty froth. Then it started pouring. They huddled cold and naked against the bushes, kissing each other's hands and drinking rain-water from the other's cupped palms, waiting for the curtain of rain to ease before pushing the canoe back into the choppy lake and paddling like mad back towards the Sugarman's boathouse.

TEN

He was standing in front of the Sugarman factory quite early Monday morning, watching the drawn faces of the workers who had gathered at the padlocked gate, waiting to clock in. These faces he knew; so unlike the faces at the brunch on the Sugarman's deck. Most already had their time cards between fist and thumb, prepared for clocking in, and it struck Bret as grotesque. In six months, they'd be standing on the same spot, but on jagged snow and ice in 30 below weather, holding their time cards in gloves or mittens and stamping their feet.

Bret had things to do in the city, and he ran over them in his mind while waiting at the factory gate for Mr. Sugarman's arrival: He had to go to Rob McMaster's to check the boxes of 'records' that had been delivered from Morocco. He supposed the merchandise had to be unpacked, sliced and weighed; and then arrangements had to be made to move it. He hated the idea of doing that work – having direct contact with the goods – something he had always dreamt of being able to avoid since his days standing in front of the Timothy Eaton statue selling nickel bags, being vigilant of narcs.

In the afternoon, he wanted to visit his mother. He had asked Tracie to fill a prescription for her and wanted to make sure that it had been delivered. He also had some money to give his mother, even some for Carl, and he rehearsed different ways in his head of telling his mother about his relationship with

Sandra Sugarman. He'd never once talked with her about his love history, as she called it, because whenever she made inquiries about girls and his relationships – a foreign word to him – he sluffed her questions off. None of those girls had anything to do with love anyways.

He thought of all those things while waiting at the factory gate for Mr. Sugarman to drive up in his Lincoln Continental. Bret had arrived embarrassingly early, but the sun was already warming up the pavement. He knew it would be awkward being alone with Mr. Sugarman because they had yet to have a private conversation.

Mr. Sugarman arrived, in a pressed suit and immaculate white shirt, saying 'fuck this' and 'fuck that' about everything, a very fluent abuse that he'd held in check at the cottage. His string of complaints began in reaction to questions from employees before he reached the gate; you could tell he hated when people squawked.

Once inside the factory, which was cool and smelled of damp, the first thing Bret saw of note was a mouse pressed flat as a flower to a bale of fabric, which caused Mr. Sugarman to laugh. Then, his arms opened wide, he darted between the bales and machines, oozing cynicism:

– This is me. My every day.

Bret kept pace as best he could while Mr. Sugarman shouted out the names of workers, the names of machines, still saying 'fuck this' and 'fuck that.' Mr. Sugarman's assistant, Abe Polanski, his collar saturated with grime, accompanied them, briefing Mr. Sugarman over his shoulder.

– This is Abe. He has my ear, and the common touch. He can waggle both of his. His father had a dairy.

The eyes of the workers were bleary, their expressions bleak as they stood by their machines waiting for the day to start. These were the faces Mr. Sugarman saw every day on his dash to austere cubby-holed offices.

A bell rang and everyone sat down in unison, like kids at their desks at school after singing *Oh Canada*, and in a matter of minutes they and their machines were racking up whizzing and clacking sounds. In his colourless office, soundproofed against the annoying commotion of the factory floor, except when the door opened, Mr. Sugarman tossed darts at Bret's forehead in the form of questions:

– Do you know anything about fabric?

– No.

– Full form? Grading? Markers? Flat sketches?

– No.

– Anything about tailoring? Cutting cloth? Apparel?

– Nothing.

– And design?

– Less.

– What do you know?

– Business, Bret said.

– I hope better than your father. Morris was a good man but no match for Gilman. You a college graduate? You study commerce?

– I've audited some courses.

– What do you do?

– Nothing right now.

– What do you live on?

– Savings.

– How did you accumulate your savings?

– Business. I know about business.

– What kind of business?

– Import-export. I worked for Max Shanus. The lawyer. He owes Shanus Imports.

– Shanus the Anus we called his father. He and his father are both lucky the *zaida* came before them. Should I ask importing/exporting what?

– You can ask.

– 'Import-export' is good enough, said Mr. Sugarman. I just need something to tell friends and family. Do you know what this job pays?

– Don't care.

– You look like a smart kid. Do you like the zoo?

– Sure.

– Do you like monkeys?

– Why?

– Do you think you could make monkeys out of those people?

– Which people?

Mr. Sugarman cocked his head towards the factory beyond the ribbed glass windows of the office partition walls.

– The toilers, Mr. Sugarman said. – Could you make monkeys out of them? The sons of toil.

Bret didn't know what to say to that; selling pot didn't make a monkey out of anyone. No one complained they were ever too high. Pot was illegal, but Bret felt morally one up.

Mr. Sugarman continued:

– You look fit for this.

– Sorry?

– I mean you look like a smart kid. You know, I think you could. What do you think?

– Could what?

– Make monkeys out of them.

– I think I could.

– But you'd have to work like a slave, Mr. Sugarman said.

– Like the monkeys?

– Yeah. But in here, not out there. That is how it is. Just say if I'm stripping this of the romance?

'In here' against 'out there' was like the division between Heaven and Hell, for monkeys, thought Bret.

– You've got four phones, said Bret.

– I could do five. You can start today.

– I have the cottage till the end of August, Bret said. – It's the first holiday I've had. Ever. Give me till September?

– Import-export, eh? Can you stay today at least? I have a supplier coming. You can watch me make a monkey out of him.

– I'm busy today.

– I hope you're not going to make a monkey out of me.

– My mom's not too well.

– What's wrong with Sally?

Bret was surprised that Mr. Sugarman knew his mother's name, and the way he mentioned it made him think that he knew more than her name.

– She's a shut-in, Bret said.

– She was a lady once. Morris was lucky to marry her. All the guys wanted her. Can I ask Abe to get you anything? It's hot in here already.

– A Coke?

– Aren't you hot?

– Why?

– Abe, get us some Cokes. It's hot in here. And check Silvia's Juki. She says the buttons come up loose. And open a window.

– On it.

– I think there's a toilet plugged in the men's convenience.

– That was fixed on Friday, Abe said.

Deft with a long, brass, pole hook, Abe crooked the ring of a tall clerestory window and it flopped forward and more noise than air rushed in. Then Abe left after scooping dimes out of a large dish for the Coke machine.

– Here, kid. Look at this fast, before Abe comes back. He's the *yachna.*

Mr. Sugarman opened his desk and took out a silver plaque with his name engraved on it. The header showed a scimitar with a gold hilt and a silver blade swinging a lemon crescent with a Pharaoh's head dangling a five-point gold star. Under the symbol Bret read: Ancient Arabic Order of the Nobles of the Mystic Shrine (A.A.O.N.M.S.).

– You're a Shriner? Bret asked.

– Nobody else knows. Not even Abe. And he has my ear.

Bret didn't know how to react to Mr. Sugarman's trust. He hadn't expected it, didn't need it, but felt complimented by it.

– Are you an Arab now? Bret said. Or a Muslim?

– I'm a Freemason. But it's hush-hush, pulling a red fez with gold tassels out of a drawer. This is a *tarboush* or a fez, he said. – I have my own fez maker. I recently converted. I'm completing my initiation.

– Do you go to a Shriner church?

– We call it a Lodge, or a Mosque, or a Temple.

– Do you drive around in a little car?

– I will. The Shriners are dedicated to fun, friendship, brotherly love, relief and truth.

– If they see you in that little car, it won't be secret.

– Nobody recognises what they don't expect.

– I can see that.

Mr. Sugarman dipped his head into the drawer again and pulled out several photographs of Shriner mini-cars.

– Which do you prefer? The mini-Corvette or the Kena 500? Or the Mustang?

– The Mustang.

– It's either air-conditioning for Abe and me or one of these cars.

– Tough decision.

– I recently made a secret pledge to the Supreme Being: we go under the Scottish rite. John Wayne was a Shriner, you know, Mr. Sugarman said.

– What kind of pledge?

– Relief. One of the five Shriner things we are dedicated to. To help someone in need.

– In import-export?

– I have chosen you. I was thinking about helping that prick of a nephew of mine. Despite what his father did to me. If you knew.

– Marty?

– But what help does he need? He's already a dirt bag on his own. He was born a dirt bag. His brother was a good kid. *Shtik* gold. I never understood that. I know Marty's a friend of yours, but he's a real dirt bag. You watch out.

– I will.

– I'm opening my business and family to you. On one condition.

– I have to become a Shriner?

– You'd have to convert to Freemasonry. But my condition is first you become pure of heart which is, by the way, what becoming a Freemason is about.

– Does that exclude import-export?

– You tell me.

– I'm guessing 'yes.'

– What about being Jewish? You won't be Jewish if you convert.

– Nobody would know. Is there anyone easier to make a monkey out of than a Jew? Who else would mistake a shower for a gas chamber? And I'm not making fun out of that.

– Do I have to convert now?

– You can take your time. But you do have to become pure of heart.

Bret had the sensation that what was happening was not really happening. It was like a high that burrowed into the brain, curled tight, then burrowed out of the brain. He saw himself looking at Mr. Sugarman and thought Mr. Sugarman was unhinged. He heard some shuffling outside the glass partition.

– Sha, *der Rebbe geht*, Mr. Sugarman said, swiftly stowing the fez and plaque away while Abe brought in two cold Cokes from the vending machine.

Bret and Mr. Sugarman sat there, sipping from their bottles. The phone rang and Mr. Sugarman said 'shit on you' and 'fuck you' a lot of times before hanging up. The only thing missing was a cigar so he could have blown smoke into the receiver.

– You won't disappoint me, will you?

– Why would I?

– Do you keep your promises?

– I try, said Bret.

Bret said he could see Mr. Sugarman driving one of those little cars, in formation, in the Shriners' Parade; they talked about that in a hush, so Abe couldn't hear. Their conversation was interrupted by another phone call, which Abe patched through this time. Mr. Sugarman while saying 'fuck' and 'shit' a lot into one receiver, picked up the receiver on a second phone and was equally forthright before hanging up both phones in tandem.

– You're in for a lot of years of doing the same boring thing, Mr. Sugarman said. This is not 'import-export'. This is everydayness.

– Import-export is routine, too. Bret said.

– You know my parents were bootleggers? Sandra tell you? They weren't the Bronfman's, and this isn't Montreal, but they knew how to make whiskey in a bathtub and then diversify before it was too late. My uncle Ernie, who was in Arbeiter Ring, a real Trotskyite, used to tell my father, *alavasholem*, that the source of all wealth is theft or exploitation. Just to irk him. Brothers. Cain slew Abel, you know.

– I wouldn't know about that, Bret said.

– You have a brother?

– Carl. Younger than me.

– Don't get rich unless he does, if you love him.

– Sure.

– He was a communist, my uncle, Ernie. A real Yid. Not one of those fake yids you see now with their little knit yarmulkes chasing you with the pledge book. Asking you to plant a forest.

– I don't know anything about that.

– I not only knew your father, but I knew all the Yeatmans, Mr. Sugarman said. Nobody liked what happened to your father. I went to B'nai Brith camp with him. Out near Húsavik. On the way to Gimli. Nothing left of it now. He was okay, your dad. He had lots of respect for people. Gilman, and his brother, too. They fleeced him anyway.

– It was his own fault, Bret said. They made a monkey out of him.

– My parlance. His friends could have helped him, Mr. Sugarman said. Gilman was an ace dirt bag. Like his brother, and his two cousins, the Feins. Royal dirt bags, all four of them. If there was a Ten of Dirt Bags, they'd have a royal flush of dirt bags. They fucked your father over, and he didn't deserve it. And yet, people should help each other: that's my philosophy, but that's not how it is. It is how it is.

– I believe that.

– And yet Gilman, he's still a friend. Ask me how come.

– Sure.

– Even in Hell, you still need friends, dirt bags or not. It's why I seek purity now. Can you blame me?

He wasn't being rhetorical.

– I can't blame you, Bret said.

ELEVEN

Like Ali Baba after stumbling into the cave of thieves and being dazzled by their riches, Bret left the Sugarman factory euphoric. All he had to do was become pure of heart, which, at the moment, appealed to him.

Feeling generously available, he drove home, to his mother's house. He had put off the visit the entire summer out of ... he didn't know what. As soon as he trod the rotted front stoop he realized that their house was atrocious. He looked at the frayed chesterfield set, which was new when they had carted it over from the house they lost in River Heights. At first an attempt had been made to entertain but no one came. Once, one Saturday night, the Kaufmans – they were old friends – came over for a drink but they'd had another party to go to and left early. Desperate and tired after that, his mother never entertained again.

His mother sitting placidly in front of the TV, which muttered and whined. A metal fan was clattering nearby on a table, alongside the smooth stones Carl brought her to paint with nail varnish. Her neck was shiny from the muggy day it had become and she had shrunk up within herself to resist it. There was a paisley tourniquet that Carl must have knotted tight around her temples to soften her headaches. She was so into her program that she didn't notice Bret was standing in the front room.

Bret took in the old person's smell, but Sally was not old. She was the same age as Ben Sugarman although she looked as grotesque as the prison she had slowly built for herself since his father had died. Life is a bad joke, he remembered him saying from his sick bed, the hospital tray jammed with medicines on the night table next to his head.

She had worked for a few years, then finally gone on welfare. Bret supplemented hers and Carl's income from his business, about which she was totally ignorant and Carl not curious. Bret made sure Carl always had sharp clothes, that the fridge was stocked and the pantry full. But he didn't rent them a cottage that summer, not even for a week or two, luckily Carl was into his friends and Bret was happy not to separate him from them during the summer lest he lose them. The sound of Tracie coming in the back door with groceries and medicine made Bret's mom raise her chin up and finally see him standing there.

– Oh, Bret. I didn't see you there. Who's in the kitchen?

– Tracie, with the groceries.

– Did she get the *yahrzeit* candles?

– It's today?

– Eight years ago tonight.

– I'm sure she did.

– Where's Carl?

– Out.

Bret made his way to the kitchen.-

– How much do I owe you? he asked.

– Thirty-four dollars and change. You can forget the change.

He pulled out his wad and peeled off a twenty, a ten, and a fin. She tried to make eye contact, which made him think she wanted a lot from him, maybe for him to be her boyfriend again if she could finally leave Max.

Back in the living room, he stood at the picture window and

watched Tracie pull away from the curb in Max's car, wondering when the best time would be to tell her about Sandra, or not at all. She had behaved properly just now and he appreciated that, feeling lucky that he had gotten off unscathed, wondering why he had been afraid in the first place. Then he sat down on the sofa with his mother, held her hand and watched her program with her. He remembered his promise to buy her a cottage, and the good luck that came with being earnest about it. Tomorrow, he promised himself, he'd go look at that cottage for sale on First Avenue and Prospect. He'd phone the realtor.

At the next commercial break, he put a half dozen eggs on to boil and returned to her side. At the following commercial break, he ran the boiled eggs under the tap. During the next commercial, he chopped the egg onto a plate with some green onions and mayonnaise, sprinkled in salt, buttered the white bread, spread the chopped egg on the bread, and cut up the sandwiches into sixteen wedges.

He lit the *yahrzeit* candle Tracie hadn't forgotten and put it in the sink so it wouldn't start the house on fire, as his mother always feared. The stainless steel of the sink turned festive and the candle seemed filled with molten gold.

He stuffed a wedge of sandwich into his mouth and carried in the plate of sandwiches in one hand and a 7-Up with ice.

– If there are sandwiches left over, run them over to Mona Joffe, his mother said. – Or Carl will eat them. Did you light the candle?

– I did.

– Did you put it in the sink? I don't want a fire.

– I did. How's Mona?

– She's better. Duddy says he's taking her to Rochester, but Duddy's a BS'er.

– I've been offered a job.

– That's nice for you, Bret.

The Sugarman factory visit had gone well, Bret thought. Although things were left unsaid, Mr. Sugarman had accepted him and he was grateful; but this fresh turn of fortune could not shake the dread that mouse plastered flat against the bale of fabric had given him. He reflected on the conversation with Mr. Sugarman about the Shriners and purity of heart while his mother munched on the sandwiches. She inquired no further into his job offer, saying only that the sandwiches were delicious and satisfying. She sipped from her 7-Up between her nibbling. The visit had become warm and pleasant, more familiar than strange, and Tracie had left without a fuss, so he had avoided turmoil. The best-case scenario would be that Tracie's feelings would run out of gas and there would never be any confrontation. He wouldn't even have to tell her about Sandra. Now that would be kismet, especially if Max never found out about him and Tracie.

– My new job is in business, he finally said. – I can afford a cottage for you.

– Import-export?

– Manufacturing. Apparel.

– People always need clothes.

– Do you know the Sugarmans?

– Ben and Lawrence? They lived on our street. Ben was a good kid. He knew your father. Lawrence liked the girls. I remember once his mother made him wear a jacket she got from Relief. It was depression times so everyone was on Relief. He screamed so hard we could hear him down the block.

– I'm dating his daughter.

– Ben's or Lawrence's?

– Ben's. He wants me to work for him. Learn the business.

– I'm not going to any engagement parties, she said.

He held her and dozed off lightly for a minute, with bread-
crumbs and speckles of boiled egg yolk on her breast.

– I saw a cottage that I want to get for you, he said.

– You don't have to buy me a cottage. Worry about yourself.
My life is over.

– Why are you saying that?

– I'm not complaining. I'm only saying.

Bret found it hard to release the grip of his mother's hand, but
he had to drive over to see Rob McMaster's new place. He went
to the kitchen and stuffed $200 in the cookie crock. He told his
mother that $100 was for Carl, some for university tuition, some
for clothes and books.

– I'm getting deliveries every day, Rob said.

Some of the boxes were already open, and chunks of greasy
hashish lay on an Ohaus scale. Normally he would never go
near so much shit, but he was anxious to ensure that the new
merchandise and arrangements were well organized. It would
be his last visit – he had no doubt about that – especially now
that he had proof of how well organized Rob could be. Later in
the afternoon, after weighing and wrapping, he took Tracie up
from the basement to one of Rob's bedrooms, the one facing
west, promising himself that he would start being pure of heart
tomorrow.

In all the bedrooms, Rob had hung the sash windows with red
chiffon drapes, and when Bret opened the door holding Tracie's
hand the bedroom looked like a red oven. Tracie's skin had an
extraordinary hue, and she felt more appealing than Sandra.

Because of the heat they made love on top of the sheets until they got thirsty. Tracie went to the kitchen and brought back a hurricane glass with ice water. After taking a mouthful, she kissed him and slowly let the cold water seep out of her mouth between his lips, onto his tongue and down his throat. She said nice things about his looks, as always, as she touched him all over, but now her touch irritated him and he couldn't wait to get into Max's car, roll down the windows, and drive with her in Max's car to a restaurant for supper. Then she drove him back to Rob's and pulled up behind his car.

Bret got out without a word. Tracie might have thought he was going back inside with her, but instead he just got into his own car, determined to be pure of heart from now on. He tuned the dial of his transistor radio to a Top 40 station that was half-way into playing 'Green Tambourine' and twisted the volume nub high.

On the open highway, his driver's window down, he accelerated in the dark after passing Fort Garry, afterburners all a go, doing 90 until he hit Matlock. He slowed to 50 and then to 30 as his headlights swept across the Winnipeg Beach sign.

Up his nostrils went the acid smells of wetlands and asphalt on gravel, cooling after a sweltering afternoon. His spirits and hopes rose. Bird and insect sounds zinged in his ears. He knew he would drive straight to his cottage, but only to wash, because there was no way he would not take off Sandra's window screen that night.

He drove up his back lane and parked on the grass in his back-yard. With a few bounds he was inside his cottage and stripping. With the rainwater from the cistern he washed his hair and torso, bending over the zinc tub until his back ached, leaving a small puddle on the floorboards. When he examined his face in the round mirror, he went back to the sink and shaved, then gave his face a strong scrub with rainwater.

He walked to the Sugarman's cottage. The moon fleshed out patches of lawn as he scratched on Sandra's bedroom screen to wake her. Her sleepy face was soon leaning against the screen, pores aligned with the fine steel mesh through which he could feel how hot her cheek was when he touched it.

In a jiffy, he had the screen off and he was sliding through the window. Her room smelled of varnished wood that had been heated all day by the sun.

– You know I could come in the front door, he said. I've been to the factory.

– Bella prefers the lie.

She embraced him with her cheek against his shoulder, where he could sniff her breath saturated with its first sleep. She led him by the hand to her bed, and hesitated.

– Put the screen back on.

– I'll just shut the window.

– I need the breeze.

He fitted the screen in place from inside, which required adroit use of fingernails and thumb tips, slightly annoyed that she had made him do this when he was hot to hold her.

– It's so hot, she whispered. How can you stand it?

– How come you sleep in your nightgown?

– Mosquitoes. They love my blood.

– Me too.

– Another letter came for you. From Liz. Do you want it?

– Not now.

– I thought you wrote her.

– I couldn't.

– She said you didn't. She's very upset. Where were you all day?

– In town.

– Import-export?

– You know I went to see your father. Why ask?

Sandra got face down on the bottom sheet, the top sheet lying in a bunch on the floor. She pulled and scrunched her night-gown up over her bum to her waist, then wriggled it up to her armpits. She had a swollen mosquito bite below one shoulder blade. Bret got naked and lay on her hot back, putting weight on his elbows so as not to crush her. Her bum felt cold though against his thighs. She reached one arm behind and pressed the small of his back with her fist; he could feel her knuckles. It was the position she'd liked when they were on their little beach, and she came in a jiffy without him. He rolled off her and onto her paperback.

– Did you lose my place?

– I folded some pages I think. Sorry.

– Next thing you know you'll be burning books.

– Did you start it over? You're on page ninety I saw. Ninety pages in a day?

– I read *War and Peace* in a month once. Don't ask me the plot.

– I don't read, he said.

– Don't or can't?

– Don't.

– So?

Her 'so?' came out of her lips without the slightest hint of contempt. He rolled back on top of her and took the book out of her hands to flip it onto her night table. His cheek was pressed to her cheek and a thick strand of her hair was trapped between them. Her lips touched the sheet, his almost did. They continued whispering.

– Can I? he asked, but her permission wasn't necessary.

– Sure. Just go in.

– Let's leave it for a minute, he said.

– Change your mind? He rolled off her again and stared up at the open rafters, quiet and thoughtful.

– What did you think of the factory? she asked. Her tone was provoking, packing a sarcastic giggle. Maybe she didn't like his increasing social success? Yet, she had led him to it.

– I met Abe, was all he said.

– He has my father's ear. My father told my mother at supper you had experience in import-export. And she believed him. She stifled another giggle.

– Your father knows the show.

– Don't make a monkey out of him. Promise?

– Are you sure I didn't hurt you before?

– If it hurt, I wouldn't do it.

– Isn't it humiliating?

– It's just playing. Just playing at it. And I like it.

– Did you take your pill?

– Are you joking?

– Yes.

– You can be clever. You might make it to the top. Of the pile.

– Pile of what?

– Ha ha.

– You thought I was dumb? he asked.

– Never. You're always sincere with me, which is like dumb to most people, so I was confused.

– You read a lot, don't you? he asked.

– If I give you some books, will you read them?

– Why don't you just tell me what's in them.

– Did you know that in Greek mythology a dead soul could choose his fate before the throne of Lachesis? Then he could come back to life.

Bret thought of his father before the throne of Lachesis. Wouldn't it be nice?

– Who was he?

– Who was *she*? Lachesis and her two sisters measured out a person's *thread of life*. Three days after your birth they knew how long you would live.

– Who?

– The sisters. The Moirai? The Fates. The Furies. Let me see: besides Lachesis there was Clotho and Atropos, right?

– You have a knack for Greek names.

– And other things Greek, she said.

– I know some Pig Latin.

– After you die, Lachesis shows you the forms you can choose from for when you return to life: people as animals, animals as people; the rich could choose to come back as the poor.

He had always thought university had to bore you to tears, but not if you heard stories like that. If the government found out what was going on, he thought, they'd stop the funding.

– How do you know all this? he asked.

– There was a witness. Er, the Pamphylian.

– Oh. Er. Of course. So the dead can choose their new fate?

– Based on their characters.

– Doesn't death destroy their characters along with their bodies?

– You're definitely not dumb. Death clarifies character by

destroying the insignificant, and then your true character can shine.

– I'll read *that* book, he said.

– What form would you choose? she asked. – After you die.

– I used to think I already died. Years ago. So you could say this is the form I chose and all this is just a dream.

– That's a defense mechanism.

– What's that?

– A defense mechanism? Dr. Sigmund Freud?

– Just summarize.

– It's when things go bad so you think it's all a dream, or things like that. I'm getting in the mood again.

– Should I?

– Just go in.

He did, and she ground her bum right and left. He had found the girl who had lived in his imagination for eight years and he didn't want things to be a dream anymore. Her breathing became panting and triggered something hard and convincing as a sneeze.

– I'm going to go, she said. – Stay hard. She chewed on the pillowcase, and he felt his atoms dancing, until they both lost consciousness.

He left just as the sun rose. He was very sleepy, and his thigh muscles were sore. He would have enjoyed waking up with Sandra, but that was something only marriage could arrange. The last thing he wanted to do was awaken Mrs. Sugarman from her lie. Ambling home barefoot along the lakeshore, his languor passed with each stride. He felt alert and content: birds sang and flitted; bugs and bees tuned up, while a droning lawnmower tore a small hole in his pleasure until the aroma of trimmed grass made up for it. The lake sparkled, and the pelicans that had already fed were preening themselves on the glitter.

TWELVE

Sandra had taken Mrs. Sugarman's Thunderbird into the city, Mrs. Sugarman told him, frowning, at their back door, the next evening. So, he went alone to the movies in Gimli.

There were two reruns playing: the first one that he watched starred Steven McQueen, but without sideburns, in *The Thomas Crown Affair*; he enjoyed everything about it: the music, the love story and Thomas Crown's opulence. The second, with Burt Lancaster, was *The Swimmer*, and he was almost alone in the theatre watching it. He sat stunned and disturbed after the credits finished rolling. If he could, he would have sat through it again because following Burt Lancaster's crushing destiny, as he swam home from pool to pool across his LA neighbourhood, aroused a pity that queerly gratified him. He wanted to feel it over again. But the projector ran out of film and the house lights came up. Emerging into the street, the marquee bulbs still blazing, his face was red with embarrassment at his own feelings. When he scratched at Sandra's screen, there was no response. He cupped his temples and looked inside, eyes slowly adjusting to the dark. Her bed was made and empty and he figured she must have slept in the city. It was the first day she hadn't been home by nightfall, and it confused him; he had a feel that things were in jeopardy.

She was back the next day and he didn't ask her where she had been so she wouldn't think he was a jealous man. After that day, she was always at home, available, lazing or reading or working around the house with her mother. She rarely touched any of the fabulous Sugarman toys – the boats and canoes – or used the pier unless he came over. None of the Sugarmans, in fact, used any of the Sugarman toys. 'It's all for show,' Sandra told him.

On the pier one sunny day, he convinced her to canoe with him to their beach and make love. A week later, Bret drove Sandra back into the city to run some pre-High Holiday errands for her mother. There was an apprehension in the air: the beach season was winding down as the harvest moon approached. There had been some crisp nights and the shocking rumour, later confirmed, that the Slonims had already put up their shutters and gone back to the city: it could be the sign for what Mrs. Sugarman called 'The Exodus,' when the Jews would flee Winnipeg Beach for the city. Then a treacherous wave of torrid air came sweeping east off the plains bringing heat under mixed skies. Some days, when Bret got into his car to drive Sandra into town, a patch of upholstery exposed to the sun burnt his thighs.

He and Sandra drove to the city past rectangles of yellow rapeseed, then neat parcels of blue flax flowers, screened off by green panels of stunted trees. He saw a swarm of grasshoppers move East with the wind and pointed it out to her.

The Falcon had bench seats so Sandra could tuck her knees under her skirt and press her body against him, hooking her arm around his right elbow, dropping her cheek on his collar-bone, but not before setting his transistor on the dashboard. She made him listen to a classical radio program on CBC. Someone was playing Chopin's preludes. He had to like them, she said, especially the Rain Drop prelude, if he seriously wanted her to love him.

He remembered that time she had been to the city earlier,

alone, in her mother's Thunderbird, and now he was hesitating about asking why she had gone. He decided not to say anything because there was no reason to interrupt his happiness. He wanted to open up to her. Tell her about his philosophy, about the promises he liked to make, about his system of rewards and punishments he used to sustain his kismet.

He didn't know what she would say to his rewards and promises approach. Would she ridicule his notions about things because she was someone who knew philosophy? She had her own, whether or not it was invented by her, or stitched together from Plato and Dr. Sigmund Freud, made little difference. He also wondered if he should tell her about his promise to Mr. Sugarman to be pure of heart and to become a Freemason in exchange for being taken into the business and the family. It seemed he could, but he was speaking to the imaginary Sandra and not her.

They ran the errands in the city. From Holt Renfrew she picked up her mother's new suit for the High Holidays, which were coming early this year, a whole month before the World Series would start, and then they picked up some dry-cleaned suits and shirts for her father at Perth's. They went to the shoe-maker's to pick up what Mrs. Sugarman called her 'sitting shoes'. Sandra had to explain that the heels were too high to walk in.

She asked him which synagogue his family used for the High Holidays. He was struck by her saying 'used,' but dismissed her curiosity about it and said that they didn't have a *shiel*. She asked why, and he said:

— People like us learn to live without a *shiel*.

— What are they good for anyway? she said. — They're just a business.

– You need a place to have a funeral.

– It's all just social pressure, she said. The High Holidays generate expectations of family feelings, then they disappoint you. This year I'll have to put up with Marty and his family. They're planning three dinners. Your family is lucky. It all stinks.

When they went shopping for steaks at Loblaw's, he used his wad of cash to pay for the groceries and wondered whether Sandra would tell her mother that he had. Then they went to pick up some things at the Polo Park Mall; he picked batteries for his radio and she picked up some books from Coles. After that, they necked in the car in the parking lot. She stopped to catch her breath.

– What do you want? she asked.

– To keep going.

– Wait till tonight, she said. – Not in the car. The steaks will go bad.

– You looked sad just now, he said.

– As sad as when Che died?

– Was Che your dog?

– Really?

– Who's Che?

– Che Guevara? Argentinian doctor and revolutionary? The Cuban revolution? Beret with a star? Big cigar? I cried when they killed him. The Americans. I do need to give you some books. You'll die for lack thereof.

The skin on his cheeks went hot and red from the shame of ignorance and also because he could have pretended to know who Che was, but he hadn't. Now he remembered the giant poster in the arcade: the man in the beret with a cigar, which was next to the Jimi Hendrix poster, and he put two and two together. He even remembered walking into the arcade to play pinball and seeing the poster of Che Guevara just as Eric Burdon howled the beginning of 'Sky Pilot.' After listening the first time to that song he was convinced the Vietnam War was evil.

— I don't have opinions, he said.

— Come on!

— You're easy to kid, he said.

— But you're not kidding. You're happy without opinions.

— You're anti-war?

She laughed at the way he put it.

— More and more, she answered.

— I am too, he said.

— There you go. That's an opinion.

He loved the smile he brought to her lips when she felt superior to him, as if it soothed her past hurts, bringing her closer to a state where she wouldn't have to be humiliated, thanks to him. He supposed someone who was more of a man than he was would be in his rights to get angry at her when he saw she was smarter or better read, but he wouldn't be that man, not even in a dream.

— You know the kids at the Beach? They're not my real friends anymore. They have no socialist consciousness.

— Marty said you lost your Jewish friends.

— Marty is grotesque.

— Are you an activist?

The word must have also sounded quaint to her: she smiled with superiority, which didn't hurt him and made him feel happy, just like he always did when he made her smile, which was never that easy or predictable.

– The steaks, she said. – It's hot in the car. And I'm a socialist, not an activist. Do you know what that is?

– Summarize.

– Do you know what the vile maxim is?

– No.

– 'Everything for ourselves, nothing for anyone else.' A socialist believes the opposite. I'm a socialist.

It sounded like a beautiful word the way she said it.

– When I'm rich, I would like to have a socialist wife, he said.

– You are funny. It's hard to know you. Were you really poor?

– There were some difficult times. No money, sometimes for days. Welfare is humiliating. It should be prohibited.

– Starvation would be better, you're saying?

– You know what I'm saying.

– The corporations get welfare, in subsidies.

– That's different. There's no humiliation involved.

He drove to her house in River Heights with the intention of dropping off the clothes and groceries. But before they got out they sat in the car with the windows down, looking at her house from the curb. It was the first time he had seen it, and he had the feeling she was showing him someone else's house, just to pull his leg.

– That's your house? he asked. The way Marty described it, it seemed like you had come down in the world.

– You should see *their* new house. It covers half of Tuxedo; they were the first Jews in, you know. They broke the barrier. Marty said it made him feel like Martin Luther King. And their cottage in Lake of the Woods is bigger than this. First Jews in there too. Social climbing in the Canadian Shield. Everest next?

The temperature had been over 80 and muggy. Thick

contorted clouds were tumbling in, their shadow licking the pavement and lawns and curbs until the sun disappeared. The atmosphere thickened with heat. Lightning flashed far away.

– It's going to storm, she said. – I love storms.

Bret, who always loved storms too, watched the sound and light show in the western sky, then he stared back at the Sugarman house. Sandra remained very still.

– It's beautiful, he said. – It's three storeys.

– It's just a house. And it's two and a half. The third storey is just to show off, until someone shows off their bigger house and you have to hide how bad you feel.

He didn't get out of the car because he thought he needed to be invited in. A blighted elm caught his attention because its boughs were already bare.

– We'd better go in. It's going to start pouring.

– Where did you go last week?

– When?

– When you came into the city alone.

– A meeting.

– What kind?

– Just a meeting. About socialism.

– Why?

– That's what socialists do. They have meetings.

– About what?

– About having more meetings.

The first raindrop smashed against the windshield. They rolled up the windows in a panic. Then they scrambled to get the grocery bags and clothes out of the car. The first hot drops fell on their shoulders and hands and then all of a sudden, the heavens opened and it poured hot water. They bolted, hangers clanking and suits in thin plastic swaying and bouncing off their hips. The storm was electrical, too. By the time they got to her threshold they were drenched, and the paper grocery bags sodden.

The downpour was deafening. Sandra got the key in the door, which was set between two lozenges of glass brick the colour of milk, and heaved it open just as tins and steaks tore through the bags and hit the marble floor of the vestibule. Sandra slammed the door behind her and hit the light switch. It was very quiet in the tiled vestibule, except for soup tins rolling towards the living room, stopping as they bumped the brass hem of white wall-to-wall carpeting. Bret, soaked to the skin, shivered because the house was like a refrigerator inside. He smelled wet paper, and the sudden change in temperature from 80 to 60 was giving Sandra multiple sneezes.

A burst of lightening made the glass brick glow, and they smiled at each other. Just like kids, when they saw the lightning they counted Mississippis until they heard the rock-splitting thunderclap, when they reached the fifth Mississippi, which meant the lightning had struck a mile away. After the next flash, which made the glass brick bright as a furnace, they could only count one Mississippi before the thunder boomed, the windows shuddered, and the lights went out.

Bret grabbed her by the waist and kissed her wet hair and wet neck as the lightening continued to illuminate the hall.

– Stop, she said. – We have to check the fuse box.

– I can't wait.

– What do you want?

– You know.

– I mean do you want to marry me?

Bret thought the guy was supposed to propose, but everyone would say it was the sixties.

– There's nothing I want more, he said. There's nothing else I want.

They peeled off their soggy clothes and rolled the length of the living room carpet until they hit a couch.

THIRTEEN

When her father came home, he found them lounging in the living room. Bret had asked her if she wanted to learn how to play Chinese checkers, but she said 'no' and lent him a copy of a pamphlet by Che Guevara on Vietnam to get through, saying: 'Here. You have a brain. Furnish it.' He tried to read, going over the same page several times, distracted by her naked legs and feet that she stretched and tucked in and out lying on another chesterfield.

He thought he saw Mr. Sugarman notice what he was reading, and wondered whether being against the war would be a sign of purity of heart.

Mr. Sugarman drove them in the Lincoln to Rae and Jerry's for steaks and baked potatoes. 'Why be original?' he said.

– As a kid we used to eat bread and radishes, Mr. Sugarman said.

– Get out the violin, Sandra said.

– Are you ready for dessert?

– Are there radishes?

– Are you staying in town for the night? Mr. Sugarman asked her. – The roads are slippery. And buckle up. Seatbelts are made to be used.

– We're going back, she said. – Mom wants me to go golfing with her in the morning.

– Nobody wants to play with her, her father said.

– She thinks it's croquet. They get tired waiting for her. She should stick to mahjong.

– Your mother was a good player, Mr. Sugarman said to Bret.

– She still has her tiles, Bret said. But she's a shut-in.

Mr. Sugarman was surprised when Bret picked up the cheque, as surprised as Bret was by the amount, underlined twice. Then Mr. Sugarman brought them home and while he got ready for bed they got the steaks out of the fridge, bagged them with the other groceries, and loaded up Bret's car. All the provisions meant Mrs. Sugarman would buck The Exodus.

The storm hadn't cooled the city, only made it clammier, but still, the ferocity of the storm had been one of those August signs that summer was fading. Another storm would come, maybe tomorrow night, maybe in two days. Then another, to suck the heat out of the last hot day, and it would no longer be beach weather, and everyone would board up their cottages. People would start buying school supplies and clothes for September, and children would get excited about going back to school, which is what he remembered he'd felt before his father's catastrophe, but not after.

Sandra sat pressed against him on the bench seat of his car, her ear on his collarbone, and he felt his good luck had been confirmed by Mr. Sugarman's tone of concern and care during supper, a concern which, in his imagination, he had projected onto Rob McMaster. He thought he'd tell Max Shanus to let Rob McMaster take over his activities when he went to work for Sandra's father. The fantasy enlarged to include putting away something of his new salary every month until he'd saved up the money to buy his mother a cottage; and also help out Carl. He was blending his promise to his mother into his promise to promote Rob into his promise to Mr. Sugarman to be pure of heart.

When they arrived back at the cottage, they found Sandra's

mother exuberant, playing mahjong with friends in the front veranda. Insects were furiously buzzing, trying to penetrate the screens, and mahjong tiles were clacking. It was a familiar sound because his mother, when they had been well off and she was still socializing, used to play with the same enthusiasm. Sally had been fearsome as a player and as an organizer of games. There were women back then who were afraid they'd be excluded from her mahjong nights.

Sandra stowed tins in the cupboard, and Bret put the steaks and vegetables in the crisper. She took his hand, put a finger to her lips and steered him cautiously to the edge of the veranda to spy on the game. A few lucky moths had snuck in and were spinning and flapping like maniacs inside the shade of the overhead lamp that illuminated the marble table. Bret noticed that one of the women arranging her tiles was Phyllis Ross's mother, Jeannette. He wondered whether she recognised him, whether the Rosses had enjoyed living in their old house in River Heights. The Rosses had bought it fair and square. Good for them. He was proud of his tolerance, what his father called fair play, and how he could repress his resentment. It was a thought about himself he'd like to share with Sandra, but it was just vanity. Between mahjong moves, Mrs. Sugarman's friends commented on their friends, especially about Mrs. Lillman's new hair colour.

— Too brash? Ida Spielman, a large slow woman, said sarcastically. She was a blonde already anyway.

— Right, blonde, said Mrs. Sugarman. — From shock.

— She's aggravating, Jeanette Ross said. One bam.

— I'm discarding the white dragon, said Leslie Boxer, queenly and pale.

They had fun with Mrs. Lillman for a while till they got around to the Aaron do.

– I'm not going out of obligation, Ida, Mrs. Sugarman said. – I'm not putting the shutters up for that. I *regretted* right away.

– That's a first, Ida said. – Are you melding, Bella? Don't tell me.

– Why do I have to go to every do?

– Come on. You're dying to go and you know it. Are you saving dots?

– I hear Sadie Bellman wasn't invited, said Leslie Boxer.

– Now there's someone who was dying to get an invitation, said Mrs. Sugarman. – It's just an obligation for me. You have to go, you go. I have zero interest. And I'm not closing up the cottage early for it. This heat wave is making Mitzi Slonim look ridiculous.

– She looked ridiculous before it, Ida said. – I'm still waiting for the red dragon.

– It'll just be you and the Zalmans left out here if you don't close up, Jeannette said.

– The Brooks invited us over again, Mrs. Sugarman said. – Third time this year. To the city! Ben wants to go out of pity. We've never said 'yes.'

– How ridiculous! Ida said. – They're after you.

– I *regretted* right away. I don't put those things off.

– Have you ever gone over there? Leslie asked.

– I know the house, said Jeannette.

– It's the one that looks good from the outside, said Ida.

– Never. They don't get it. They'll invite anybody, just to get a quorum. Teachers, accountants. Luckily I'm out here all summer. It's so beautiful here. The nature.

– The days are getting shorter, Leslie said, dreamily.

– They're still 24 hours last I heard, said Mrs. Sugarman. – And I'm not closing the cottage because of the Aarons. Or for the Slonims.

With that, Mrs. Sugarman was creating a countertrend. While it was the snobbish thing of late to shutter the cottage early, in mid-August, she had decided to stick it out till the end of August, buck the trend, see how far that got her, and see how people would talk about that. And if that meant snubbing the Aarons, it might work.

– I can't stand them, Sandra said to Bret, raising her arms high. – Can't hack her. The Zalmans are staying until Labour Day. It really irked her when she found out. Now she appreciates nature. Soon she'll be a hippy.

– Why?

– There are things happening in the world. Serious things. No one she knows has a socialist consciousness. Everything for themselves! Everything is about them. She laughs and cries with the same face. Like a bad actor. Did you hear how she used that word?

– What word?

– *Regretted.* Didn't you hear it? Regret as a verb. Talking like she's educated but she's not. I won't end up like her. I'll make sure of that. We'll make sure. This didn't happen to Leonard Cohen in Greece.

Bret wanted to defend Mrs. Sugarman, but a war between mother and daughter might upset Sandra's status and his plans. Instead, he looked out at the lake in the moonlight. The wintry glint on the water brought him down.

FOURTEEN

The next day before noon he went to the drugstore to call Rob, and then Tracie, to ask about Max and things Moroccan. He wished he hadn't called her; it put him in a dreary mood. The heat in his body became so unbearable that he went home and washed his hair with cold rainwater. Cooling his scalp restored him. It must have been the hottest day in August, or for the year, and it made him chuckle at how preposterous the Slonims were looking for closing up. He smiled at the relish Mrs. Sugarman must be feeling. The radio said some farmers were desperate because the earth was cracked and parched and the brief but nasty thunderstorms here and there weren't helping. Bret had always worried about things like that, about the farmers and drought, and wondered if that was having what Sandra called a socialist consciousness. The radio said heavy clouds were blanketing Brandon and he wished for them to cross the entire province with a slow benign rain. But storms were more likely. There were some sports scores given, and a report of the number of Viet Cong killed the day before.

Sandra appeared at the door to his veranda in blue thongs and a white cotton sundress that fell against her knees. She was knocking softly from courtesy, because she just opened and came inside, letting go carelessly of the screen door behind her so it snapped back loudly into the frame.

Like his, her hair was wet, just combed, and she reminded him of a child ready for bed.

– You didn't come over this morning, she said.

He was still drying his hair and chest and looked at her before wrapping the towel around his neck.

– I thought you should know that I was taken advantage of once, she said. – That's rape.

Coming from Sandra's lips the word made him shudder, although the story wouldn't be a surprise in her case.

He also knew girls who had been taken advantage of, but he hadn't heard it from them.

– I just told you something, she said.

Despite the heat in the veranda, he felt chilled; he realized she was going to talk about it. Any second now. He thought about what he could say before she began, to cut her short, then he thought he wouldn't say it, but then he did:

– I know. Marty told me. – But he said he jumped you. He didn't say he raped you.

She used her fists on his chest like she was banging on a door in a dream: her blows had energy but no effect on him.

– You know? You know? Marty told you?

– Stop hitting me.

– Why didn't you tell me you knew?

– Stop hitting me.

– Alright. I will, she said, before slapping his cheek so hard his head turned.

– Was I supposed to tell you I knew? he asked, sincerely.

– Didn't it make me disgusting?

– No.

– Did you laugh together?

– No.

– How could you have touched me after you heard that?

– I was hoping it was just Marty's BS.

– It wasn't. How could you even touch me?

Bret was frightened that she would love him less or not at all because he had tolerated what Marty had done to her. He knew this feeling she was having: loath to love someone who thought less of you. But she was angry for a different reason that he realized he was might be too dense to understand. Because he stayed silent, she continued.

– Are you sick? Some sort of pervert?

– Why?

– Don't you find rape revolting?

– Yes. And I find the rapist revolting, not you. I should have smacked him.

– You don't find me revolting? That's sick. We were having sex, and all the time you knew.

– It didn't make you revolting.

– I'm talking about after Marty told you.

– Why would I find you revolting?

– Disgusting?

– No.

– Well, that's disgusting.

– You got over it, Bret said. – Marty said you didn't hold a grudge.

– Next you'll be saying that I showed character!

– Didn't you? His face felt horrible and sweaty, like a dog had slobbered on him. – That means you fought him hard. He said you kneed him.

– Did you just say that as if I'm a hero?

– You fought hard.

– And if I hadn't? If I had just gone numb from fear right away?

– That's different.

– How? Tell me how.

Bret couldn't think of how.

– So you think I'm a hero, she said. – Like Valentina Terechkova?

– Who?

– The first woman in space. Forty-eight orbits.

There was something awry: she was angry because he hadn't been disgusted by her all this time. That didn't make sense to him because he wasn't. Was she trying to break up with him? The fear of rejection made him very frightened.

– I don't think less of you for any of that, he said.

– I think less of me for that.

– You're you. But you didn't let him rape you.

– You can't let someone rape you. It's an oxymoron.

He remembered as a kid that he thought an oxymoron was the worst type of moron, but Max Shanas had disabused him of that definition while teaching him what *disabuse* meant, and it wasn't the opposite of abuse.

– Marty said you fought back as long as you could.

– I didn't want to have sex with him. I kicked him hard. I kneed him. And he slapped me. But that's not why I gave in.

– It's okay now. I don't want to hear anymore.

– All this time, making love, and you knew this about me. You're a pervert.

– I'm not a pervert.

– Freud says all men are perverts.

– Why?

– So that's why I like it the way you call 'humiliating.' Because I was never raped there.

He felt a vein beating in his right temple from having to filter too many fears at the same time, the biggest being that she had come over with the idea of breaking up with him and this argument was just a pretext.

– He raped my brain first, you know. Then he pinned me down. Slapped me some more. But the hitting didn't get me in the mood. After, I told him I forgave him. He convinced me to do that, too, because I had dated a lot, he said. He had always ridiculed me for dating too much. He said I should think about what he did as if it was just like one more date. So now you know. Now you know me.

– I never asked for more than that, Bret said.

She thought about that. He could tell it came unexpected to her. He had the sensation that what he just said made him intelligent in her eyes.

– Luckily, I was on the pill, she continued. – It was disgusting. Getting raped not only by force but by being, what? Is there a word for it? Duped. Duped raped? Maybe. And all because I forgave him. Really disgusting. Really filthy. And what it makes you.

– Do you want me to go?

– This is your cottage.

– So what. Do you want to go?

– Maybe. Maybe not. I don't know why I started telling you this. I'm actually really shy. I never talk at meetings.

His dazzling panic that she had come over to break up with him lessened as she turned so meek that he felt reprieved. So what was going on?

– I think I should go, she said.

He looked at her and sensed she wanted him to feel revolted by her, or at least say that he did. For what purpose? He had to think carefully of what to say, but nothing came out, except:

– Don't go.

– Can I have a glass of water? My armpits are soaked. I stink.

– You don't stink.

– Say something to me, she said.

All he had to do was say the right thing and their intimacy would rise to a new place, one so private that it would bind them together in secrecy and shame, a state equivalent to her getting pregnant and having to marry him. He would instantly catch up to everyone. Yeah. It was like that. Nevertheless, he didn't feel he was in control of things, and couldn't come up with the right thing to say.

Not far from him she stood – like her father did sometimes – her feet spread and planted firmly, fists on her hips, her chin proud. He couldn't help positioning himself behind her and rolling up her dress to her navel. Then she kicked her thongs hard off each foot, right across the room, shattering the water glass that stood by the zinc tub.

– Do you want to know the details? she asked.

– No.

– Sure?

– Why?

– I can tell you if you want.

He didn't answer. Then she asked him something. He refused, several times, then relented. They made love, but not with love, and it lit things up for both of them.

FIFTEEN

From inside the car, he saw Tracie standing in Max's picture window, smiling, watching him scrape the curb with his hubcaps, reverse and adjust his parking. He didn't wave to her until he was loping up the busted front walk. She had business news from Max and they discussed it in the living room, on Max's beige chesterfield, focusing on Max's instructions: he would be back the next Wednesday and had asked her specifically to make sure it was Bret who picked him up at the airport.

– Want a fast game? she asked.

– Where's the board?

They played Chinese checkers and had fun till they got tired of it and left the last match unfinished. They moved to Max's untouchable long red couch and began smoking hash with Max's hash faucet. Tracie had her shoulder blades against the upholstered arm, her knees up, making a teepee over Bret's lap. Achieving purity of heart would be hard today, but he'd try.

– Should we go up? she asked.

– Is this a habit?

She bent forward to kiss him but he waved her away.

– Please? she said. – Don't be like that.

Saying 'please' that way made her eyes larger and darker, and she underlined it by scuffing her bare calloused heels on the waxy velvet. Bret thought that she might scratch or tear the fabric if she continued. Okay, he said to himself. Go upstairs and make love to her lightly, lightly, lightly, then leave as if nothing happened and that will make it be as if it hadn't happened.

– There's something new I want to try, she said.

– Max will be back in town soon.

– Not tonight.

– Soon.

– I want to try it with you first. You need to shave.

He succumbed and she went upstairs, straight to the sunroom. Bret went to Max's bathroom on the main floor. He couldn't resist looking at himself in the mirror while he soaped his cheeks. He thought there was a depravity in his look and not a trace of purity. Using Max's razor, he shaved closely so he wouldn't give her a rash. When he finished he looked cleaner and rinsed the last streaks of soap off his face, thinking that now he wouldn't look so depraved before making love.

– Said and done.

His voice sounded cheerful when he told Tracie to get undressed. He now looked forward to making love to someone who didn't think he was perverted.

Tracie got undressed, looking at him with respect and affection, perhaps with the respect that she showed Max? He felt flattered, his spirits raised, and he realized it was his birthday, something he had kept hidden from Sandra because birthdays, which made you the centre of attention, embarrassed him.

– Why don't you take over the business from Max? Tracie asked. – I think he wants out. He wants to have kids.

– Never thought about it. Besides, I have something else going on.

– What?

– You'll see.

– I bought you something, Tracie said.

– What is it?

– For your birthday. Didn't you get any presents today?

– Birthdays don't mean much, he said.

– Birthdays are important. She drew forth a thin Eaton's box from under a pillow. Out of the tissue she lifted a fine leather wallet and showed it to him.

– It's real leather, she said. Inside the wallet there was a slip of paper with a girl's name and telephone number.

– Who's Terri? Bret asked.

– A friend. She wants to meet you. You want to meet her?

– I'm thinking about it.

– So?

– I'm not sure.

– Not sure of what?

– I have to be pure of heart.

– Why?

– It's a promise. But I'm not sure if it includes sex or excludes it.

– Should I call her?

– Now?

– Why not?

– Would she come over?

– Should we start?

– Let's go back down.

They flipped through magazines in the front room while they waited for Terri to drive over. When they got impatient they went outside to wait for her on Max's stoop. The sky was flush with stars and teeming with insects. He promised himself that he would start being pure of heart for sure the very next day because he had decided that purity of heart had to include sexual fidelity to Sandra. He would have promised Sandra supreme fidelity if that were possible, but there were no gradations to fidelity, he thought. He would start tomorrow. Tonight he promised himself that he'd moderate his pleasure with Tracie and Terri so that the pleasure he got from Sandra would never be eclipsed.

   – I know you, Terri said. – I know him, she said to Tracie.

On the stoop he dimly recognized her face – her eyelashes were like a giraffe's – but he couldn't place from where. He thought maybe he'd seen her at The Ting, listening to folk music, or singing it. He was embarrassed that she knew him better than he knew her, or so she let on. She was shy, tense, strangely mature, and very likeable. But the three of them had nothing to talk about, and when that happens you have to smoke up, so they went inside.

They sucked hard on Max's hash faucet, until the red knibble glowed and turned to ash. Then Tracie lost her grip. Then Terri got giddy. Bret lost it too, as his brain flitted from apprehension to silliness. Before the giddy rush to sex began, Bret asked Terri if she was anti-war.

   – I don't follow the news, she said.

   – Wars are horrible, said Tracie.

   – It's a moral thing, said Bret. You feel it in your heart or not.

   – Bret is pure of heart, said Tracie, giggling.

   – How pure? Terri asked. Do you have a girlfriend?

   – Maybe.

   – No, he doesn't, Tracie frowned.

   – How pure are you? Terri asked him directly.

   – What do you mean?

   – For instance, do you like doing everything?

– What do you mean by everything? Tracie asked her. – He doesn't do anything strange or disgusting.

– New things that can widen your circle? Terri said straight to Bret.

– This is getting weird, Bret said.

– What circle? Tracie asked Terri.

It took time for Bret to get it, but he did. Tracie was taking her time. Terri was already laughing into her knuckles watching Tracie trying to catch up.

– What circle? said Tracie. – You guys! What circle?

They both laughed again, without Tracie, who got miffed.

– Circle of friends? Tracie asked. – What circle?

Tracie then got wise, smiled and bonked Terri on the head, then noogied her; it made them all giggle and get hash hiccups, which provoked more giggles. Bret noticed that Terri's forehead was grainy with tiny pinpoints of old acne, as if someone flung fine salt there and it stuck. She had tried to cover it with make-up.

After the second hash nugget delivered its load and had turned gray and weightless, Tracie knocked the faucet inside the ashtray.

– Terri and I are going upstairs, she said to Bret. – You can come up after you enjoy your purity of heart a bit.

How long is *a bit?* He sat contemplating the fact that so many strange and joyous things had been happening and whether they – even the distractions like tonight – would all lead to him to driving a mini Mustang in the Shriner's parade one day. With a 'gone' head he mused on the exact origin of all these wondrous events: was it the promise he'd made to buy his mother a cottage? He felt that if he could just identify the origin of his kismet, then he could control it so it wouldn't crash.

He went upstairs to the sunroom, but no one was there. Then he went to Max's bedroom and rapped on the door with a single knuckle. From within Tracie said:

– How's your purity of heart?

– Good.

– Don't come in yet!

– What are you doing in there?

– Talking. Go away.

He nipped back and waited in the sunroom, imagining what Tracie and Terri might be doing. Out of curiosity he poked his head out the door of the sunroom just as Terri came out of Max's room. She looked older, fuller, and more appealing naked.

– You're lovely, he said.

– You're cute, too, Terri said. – Maybe even gorgeous. Or not. I was just coming to talk to you. Terri made to walk toward him and he jumped. So she stopped.

– Tracie says you should come in in ten minutes.

– Why?

– Negotiations.

– What did you want to talk about?

– I just said it, she said and went back inside.

Back in the sunroom he got through five minutes by examining the wallet Tracie had given him, but he couldn't hack another five and went inside Max's bedroom without knocking. Tracie and Terri were sitting naked on the edge of Max's hefty bed, necking. Their cheeks were pink and shiny, their knees knocking against each other's.

He made love to Terri first, while Tracie sat on the edge of the bed, shy and overexcited. Then he made love to Tracie, then Terri again. He came inside Terri first, not Tracie. Despite her red cheeks, Tracie looked defeated when she saw what he'd done.

In the morning, he was furious with himself, like a gambler who, just before sunrise, is suckered into playing showboat only to throw away all his hard-earned winnings. Was enjoying Terri and Tracie a reward, or would it bring punishment? Here it was – tomorrow – and he had a promise to keep: should he leave, begin to be pure of heart now? Or filch more pleasure from the girls? Terri and Tracie's morning scents didn't resolve the issue, but their pinning him down took away his choice.

SIXTEEN

He was back on the veranda of his cottage, happy to have left the city, listening to R&B on his radio, trying to read the Plato book Sandra had given him. It was the first cold wet day of late August and the wind blew keenly. He could hear a neighbour hammering, putting up his shutters, driving nails through the soft pine. Suddenly, the inevitability of the end of summer changed his mood.

He put on long pants and a gray and white Icelandic sweater he'd bought in Gimli. He felt not only protected from the cold, but handsome and vain enough to make him think he could read an important book – a classic – as Sandra called it. But as hard as he tried to read a chapter called 'The Allegory of the Cave,' he couldn't concentrate for more than a page or two, before thinking that the only way he could ever learn to read like Sandra, think like Sandra, was to be in prison, with guards watching to make sure he'd read every word, every page, every chapter, and understood it all.

After loading his pocket with dimes, he biked to the drugstore and in the grey chill dialled Rob McMaster's number to check on the *consignments*. Then he called Tracie to find out when Max Shanas's plane was landing. Then he called his brother to see if he had registered for university. Then he called one of his pushers, Gord, who worked the Timothy Eaton statue like he used to, to tell him to be careful of the 'back-to-school' narcs. On an impulse, he called Mr. Sugarman to ask him about Freemasonry and what *purity of heart* meant, exactly.

– Hold the line, Bret, would you?

He heard Mr. Sugarman say 'fuck this' and 'fuck that' to someone in the office, or maybe into one of his other phones.

– Sorry, Bret, but everything is going to shit. With or without me. And the High Holidays are breathing down my neck. I hate them. I have to take two days off next week. Abe, too. Who asked *him* to be Jewish? Purity of heart? You asked. It means don't get girls pregnant.

Mr. Sugarman, waiting for Bret to say something back, breathed and sighed impatiently: – What did you think it meant?

Bret wasn't sure it was a real question. Bret had given a sublime reading to *purity of heart*, a bridge-too-far thing, and he had thought Mr. Sugarman had too. Just in case Mr. Sugarman's question was sincere, Bret said:

– I think it means being faithful.

– It was a rhetorical question, Bret. – I've got to hang up now, but before I do, Sandra tells me you don't have a *shiel* for the High Holidays.

– That's right.

– You can sit with us. In Bella's seat. Mrs. Sugarman never sits inside for more than twenty minutes. She only comes for the blow job.

– Sorry?

– When they blow the *shofar* to send everyone home. Have you got a suit?

– I've got a suit.

This was a lie.

– Imported?

– I'm not sure. It's from Eaton's.

– I'm just kidding you. I'm hanging up now. Have you got a *tallis*?

– My father's. He had two. They buried him in his good one.

– I'm hanging up now.

As he was putting down the receiver, he could hear Mr. Sugarman say 'fuck this' and 'fuck that' into another phone.

Back at the cottage, he had just started reading the book again when the best and final distraction of the morning arrived. Sandra, cupping her temples, peered in at him through the screen. She was wearing a black cashmere sweater, and he thought, with unchecked joy, how tender it would be to neck on the chesterfield and feel her up under her sweater. If she let him, he promised himself he'd tell her about Tracie and Terri. Maybe it would make her feel less guilty about having been duped. She went to use the bathroom and he continued reading while he waited for her.

– I had to put in my diaphragm, she said. – My mother dragged me into town to get it.

– I thought you got one with Liz.

– I couldn't tell her I already had one. Now I have two. A two-diaphragm girl. 'No more abortions, please,' she said to me in the car. Can you believe it?

– Did she go with you to Montreal when you had it? You never said.

– Of course. All mothers do the Montreal thing if they have to. Don't you know? I don't come from a family that goes to Montreal, or anywhere else, for any reason.

– My head is aching.

– Do you want me to rub it? she asked. – What are you reading?
He showed her the book.
– What do you think? she asked. – Did you read the myth of
the cave?
  – I didn't understand it.
  – Come with me.
She took him to the bedroom, the one where he seldom slept.
It was stuffy and he would have liked to open a window and
flap out the stale air, but she drew the thick green drapes in two
jerks and shut the door to make it pitch black. They stood in the
dark for a minute. He couldn't see her but he could smell her
and wanted to kiss her, put his hand up her sweater, and touch
her naked back.
  She switched on a lamp with a cone shade that was on the
night table and turned it on its side: a crisp disc glared on the
wall. She forced him to sit on the edge of the bed and look at it
while she huddled on his lap. Then she projected finger puppets
onto the white disc: first a wolf that opened and closed its mouth,
its tongue vibrating. She whispered in his ear as he stared at the
shadow puppets she made:
  – Imagine all your life you're imprisoned in a cave with others
and all you saw was shadows on a wall projected by torches
behind you. One day you escape and see the world. When you
return to the cave you tell the others that their world isn't real,
but they don't believe you. Well, for Plato, the world of shadows
is our world, and we do not, nor will we ever, know the real
world. Ergo: human reality is only human perception.
  – I've had thoughts like that before reading your book. Sometimes I've felt that this is all a dream.
  – I know. You told me. Your defense mechanism.

– Why didn't you tell me that I felt what Plato felt? You paint him like a sort of genius.

– Platonism is the source of Western culture, she said. – Where reality is perception, and ultimately not real. But I'm against that.

These thoughts were too deep, and he thought he'd appreciate them better if he were holding her down by her shoulders and kissing her neck and up under her jaw and behind her ear. They made love in the musty bedroom, and instead of having to turn her on her belly right away she asked him to tell her about the other girls he had made love to before her, including Liz.

– I can't do that.

– Come on.

Was it a trap? he wondered. But she was breathing too hard for that, so he told her a story that she could *think* he was making up, or not, about Tracie (using her real name), albeit moving the action from yesterday into a deeper past. When he told her about Tracie and Terri together he also projected them into the past. Her reaction was intense: she started panting harder from excitement, getting close to where she wanted to go. All of a sudden, she panicked, unable to draw a decent breath.

– Did you? she asked, looking for comfort. – Did you really do that?

– Why?

– With two girls? One watching?

– It was for kicks.

She covered her face. – You're lying, she said.

– You asked me.

Then she started panting again, recouping her excitement; through the gasping he could hardly hear her fire off her questions about it, needling him for details and confirmations. They made love like that until she said she was going to cry, and did, bursting into tears.

– Don't tell me that was a dream, he said.

– I told you I'm against that.

Afterwards she asked if any of it was true, and he swore he'd made it all up for her pleasure; and then he told himself that the relief he saw in her eyes meant that's what she wanted to hear: a lie – that was true – that was a lie.

– I'm jealous in retrospect, she said, laughing at herself. I'm such an idiot.

– What do you mean in retrospect?

– Because it happened in the past, before I knew you.

– But it never happened, he said.

They were inseparable that last week. The cooler days spaced themselves evenly. They necked once near the lake in the harvest moonlight and she said 'isn't it romantic,' just after unsticking her lips from his. In his life so far, he thought, there had always been 'something else', something to come or something to expect, but now it was all here and now.

SEVENTEEN

It was the last day of August, and his wish was not to leave Sandra's side for fear of jinxing his luck. Locals had come early that morning to put up the shutters at Sandra's cottage, and Bret pitched in to squeeze the last few hours out of the summer to be as close to her as possible. After wind and rain and a few chilly days the weather started warming, and it was hot in the sun by ten, promising even hotter weather for rest of the day and the High Holidays.

– It always happens, Mrs. Sugarman said to Bret. The hottest day is when you shutter the cottage. She was wistful and friendly and Bret wanted to say something pleasant to her, but he didn't know what, maybe never would.

Together with Sandra, he watched Mrs. Sugarman press glasses of well water into the workmen's large cracked hands when they took a smoke break on the deck. The Sugarmans were the last to pack it in, the originality of which apparently gave Mrs. Sugarman a social edge for how she would be perceived during the High Holidays. Could anything less important be more important? Sandra asked him spitefully.

Around noon, the last shutter went up, and he got a bad feeling about it. The Sugarman plan was to spend the rest of the day closing up the house: wiping down the kitchen cupboards, cutting off the water and power, packing up the car, winching the inboard to the rafters of the boathouse and covering it with a tarp. Then they would drive back to the city together to get home by seven. Bret was invited to dinner but still he felt agitated when he left her.

He had things to do, he told himself, and that relieved his anxiety. While he didn't have to shutter his rented cottage, he did have to pack up the Falcon, fit his bike in the trunk, tidy up, wash the shelves of the fridge, lock the doors and drop off the keys at Shecky Kaufman's and pay the two months of rent, which took some heft out of his wad. He also had to get into the city to pick up Max at the airport but after buying that suit he had told Mr. Sugarman he already had. To do that, he first needed to see Rob McMaster to get some cash to pay for it because the bank would be closed. Bret also wanted to keep that promise he'd made himself to secure a promotion for Rob after he quit and was toying with whether to tell Rob sooner than later. He decided on sooner.

– I'm out, by the way, he told Rob as he was pocketing the cash.

– Out of what?

– This is my last deal. The hash records. You want, you can move up.

– And Max?

– Max won't say 'no.' I promise you.

– If you need more cash, we'll be making a bundle with Labour Day coming up. It's part yours anyway.

– Keep it for now. I have enough.

At Eaton's he stood in his stocking feet in front of a full-length mirror looking at the suit on him. He picked out a gray suit so dark it was almost black.

– Sharpy-doo, said the salesman.

– It looks too new, said Bret. – The fabric feels stiff.

– Break it in.

– But I need to wear it soon, Bret said.

– When?

– What's today?

– Tuesday.

– I need it Thursday.

– Just wear it today and tomorrow all day. Do you want double cuffs? We can hem it now while you wait. Bret checked his watch: he had to be at the airport by 4 to pick up Max.

– Okay. I'll wait. How long for the cuffs?

– Twenty minutes. The lady's here now.

– I can do twenty minutes.

He wanted to tell Max right away he was out and square accounts with him and ask him to let Rob McMaster replace him because he was set to start work at the Sugarman factory on the Tuesday morning after Labour Day. He had felt good telling Rob that he would take over from him: a promise he would keep.

– You're on time! Max Shanus said to him, opening the back door of the Falcon to throw his suitcase in by the handle, pulling his hair behind his ears as he slid into the front seat.

– How was the trip?

– We're going to be rich. *Inshallah*. God willing.

Max had more kismet type words, and he used them as they drove to Max's. Despite bloodshot eyeballs and dark circles under his eyes, Max was in the mood to be pleasant. He adjusted the dial on Bret's transistor radio and changed to a Top 40 station where 'Sunshine of Your Love' was playing. Max said he could groove to it for a week and had done just that in Morocco.

– I'm going to be busy during the High Holidays, Bret said. – So I'll be off.

149

– I should put in appearance at *shiel* too. My father bought me a seat. I didn't figure you for that. Is Rob doing okay with the stuff?
– Moving kibbles. Kids and stoners getting ready for university. They'll get cash for books and new sweaters.
– *Inshallah.*
– By the way, Bret said.
– What?
Bret told him he wanted to be out of the business once the High Holidays were over.
– You can fuck off anytime you want, always could, Max said, but Bret didn't like the face he made. Bret felt his own face warp into anxiety.
Max had that weaselly knack of making the world suddenly cold and inhabitable only if you saw it as a shit place too. Now, it made Bret wonder whether Max knew about him and Tracie.
– I think Rob can take over once I'm gone, he said.
Max muttered that Bret's suggestion to let Rob take his place was doable, but not 'fait-accompli', then asked, – Did you tell him yet? he asked.
– Yeah.
– You should have asked me first.
– Seemed natural.
– I'm going to have to think about it. Wasn't your decision to make, Bret.
That struck Bret in the pit of his stomach. If he wasn't able to keep his promise to Rob, the consequences could be terrible for both of them.
Tracie was at the picture window when they pulled up and parked. After a short embrace in the front hall, Max and Tracie went upstairs to his bedroom, leaving Bret alone on the landing,

putting down Max's suitcase and not knowing what to do next. He figured he could leave. If Max had anything more to say to him about the business then he would have said it. Still, it hurt that Tracie had gone upstairs to make love to Max: it was only jealousy, he told himself, nothing unfathomable, but it bruised him too easily. Luckily he had somewhere to be.

He got to the Sugarmans' at 7:10 on the dot. Sandra and Mrs. Sugarman had left their things in the car in the driveway and they asked him to unload it for them and pile up the boxes of summer clothes and linens by the staircase. On one of his trips back and forth out to the Thunderbird he left the back door of the house open wide so that he wouldn't have to juggle the boxes in one arm every time he wanted to open the door to get back inside.

– Hey, there's air-conditioning, Mrs. Sugarman shouted before she shut the door.

After carting in the last box, he stood uncomfortably at the foot of the tall staircase wondering what to do with all the boxes he had piled there. He waited for instructions, wondering if Sandra would appear on the top stair to deliver them. Suddenly, standing there at the bottom looking up, he had a bizarre sensation that he was weary of Sandra. But how could one be weary of a dream?

He remembered that a similar feeling had taken hold of him with Liz after she got clingy and submissive. He shook the feeling off, chalking it up to the humiliation of having to swallow Mrs. Sugarman's crack about the air-conditioning.

Minutes later, Sandra bounded down the stairs, two at a time, grabbed his arm and pulled him enthusiastically up to her bedroom. That fixed his mood.

– I'm going to model for you, she said.

– Model what?

He sat on the slippery white bedspread on her big bed while she walked between him and her full-length mirror in her new black suit for *shiel*, her legs clad in mother-of-pearl stockings.

– What do you think?

Then, for no reason, he asked if he could pay for her suit, and she said that would be a vulgar thing to do, but he didn't know why she said that and didn't get why it was vulgar.

– I bought a new suit, too, he said. – I didn't want to wear my old one.

– Show me.

She made him fetch his new suit from his car. He tried it on for her in front of her mirror and she said it fit well, too well; he was sure he looked good in it too, and she noticed that. He heard a slight irritation in her voice as she said:

– I never realized you enjoyed looking at yourself.

– Me?

– Just now.

– I like the suit, he said. – 'I should have bought two,' as my mother would say when she liked something on her.

Sandra started undressing. After hanging up her suit, she lay on her elbows on the bed in her bra and panties and stockings, just looking at him. He was stuck standing by the mirror in his new suit, not knowing whether to take it off or not.

– I'm going to Minneapolis for an anti-war demonstration, she said.

– When?

– This weekend.

– Who with?

– Some friends.

– Beach friends or Socialist friends?

– Anti-war friends. Americans.

He waited, confused, lacking information he should have already had.

– Americans?

– From Minneapolis.

– What's wrong? she asked, noticing his concern. You hate Americans?

– Not until now.

He was sure she thought he was jealous about Minneapolis. He wasn't, not like he was when he saw Tracie go upstairs with Max. He was just afraid his good luck would come to an end if she went so far away: that a separation would jinx things. It was this fear that was making him pull a jealous face. To repress it, he told himself he liked the fact that she would be doing good for the world. He needed a few days anyway to wind things down with Max and Rob, and Tracie: he'd finally tell Tracie he had a girlfriend and that he could never make love to her again. Severing all those ties would be the sacrifice he would make for becoming *pure of heart* as he defined it, not as Mr. Sugarman defined it.

– What's wrong? she insisted. – Are you afraid I might sleep with someone in Minneapolis?

– Are you going there to protest or to make love? Because you don't have to go to Minneapolis to make love, or cheat.

– It would just be for fun.

– You trying to make me jealous? he asked.

– Maybe. You look frightened.

– You can't make me jealous because I'm never jealous, he said.

– I can't imagine you enjoying sex with anyone more than me.

– Did you make that up? she asked.

– Would you drop me because I'm not jealous?

– Will *you* sleep with someone while I'm gone? she asked.

He thought she had put him in the mood to play dirty with her; so any answer to that question would be her fault.

– Maybe, he said.

– Maybe with who?

– On such short notice? he asked.

– Yeah.

– It couldn't be someone new. I don't like going to meat markets. It'd have to be someone easy. Maybe Tracie or Terri.

– I thought you made them up. You said you made them up.

– They're real.

As she sat forward he saw her armpits were slick, and when she realized that too she took off her bra and used it to wipe them before flinging it across the room.

– But that's not what you swore, she said, panicky.

– It happened last week. Not in retrospect.

– You cheated on me?

– It was just for fun.

– Are they prettier than me?

– Put together, he said.

– Was that just a compliment?

He could see that Sandra didn't know whether to strike him or kiss him.

– And here I was. Trying to make you jealous, she said. – This is worse than being duped. You're killing me. I could punch you hard.

– You could call your mother up to hit me too.

– She's the one always defending, you know! She told my father to be nice to you. Employ you. We're all nice to you.

– I'm grateful.

She got off the bed and bore down on him. Her fists and teeth were clenched, and she shivered abruptly to flush out her rage, sucking in spurts of air through tight lips, but Bret thought that just around the corner from her exasperated face there was a smile you suppress before being caught in a lie..

The weariness he had felt earlier for her, that Liz Kowtun-weariness, vanished. Everything now depended on having her, on her being his captive if need be.

– I want you forever, he said. – This is forever. Minneapolis means nothing.

She didn't care that her mother was home and might hear them; her door had a lock and she bolted it before yanking his suit sleeve towards the bed. He resisted and she yanked it again. Raising his free arm as she pulled the other, he made a show of relenting.

– Okay, okay.

He took skidding steps forward to the bed as she tugged, followed by two aggressive strides. He turned it into her rescue by now grabbing her by her wrists, lifting her off the floor and dropping her down on the bed on her bum.

– I'm not going to Minneapolis, she said, squeezing his body from underneath, looking up into his face. – I changed my mind. Happy?

– You want to turn over?

– No. I want to look at you.

He couldn't help smiling. He was just that relieved and happy that out of her desperation she didn't want them to be separated, and that his plans might just work after all. So he proposed to her. He thought she'd say 'no', but she said 'yes.'

This 'yes' was a hole down into which went the entire island of Phraxos.

– Should we tell your mother now? he asked while they dressed.

– We can tell my parents after *shiel* tomorrow. – Don't get there early. Eleven is fine. You'll be bored.

– I've been to *shiel* before. I know how boring it is.

– Make it 11:30.

– You think they'll be okay with the engagement?

– After my mother went with me to Montreal people found out and then I wasn't engaged any more. I think anything makes them happy for me now. The bar has dropped.

– As low as me?

– They're my parents. What can I do about them? I want to go to Mykonos for the honeymoon. I can be in control of my life there.

– Why not Phraxos?

– There is no Phraxos. It's made up in the book.

– How was I to know?

– It's all pleasure there. Because it's not here. There's no high and no low.

EIGHTEEN

Y ou look pleased, Max said to Bret.

He had finished up a long meeting with Max and Rob about winding up his involvement in the business and everyone was happy, especially him. Max's hesitation about replacing him with Rob had only been Max teasing him. Bret's share of the money from the Moroccan imports could go to a down payment on that cottage for his mother. End of the season was always good time to buy: catch them after their cottages have been shuttered.

Bret was still wearing his suit, breaking it in so it wouldn't creak tomorrow at *shiel*. Max ribbed him about his duds, but Bret had thought the suit would give him confidence and say-so with Max. The ribbing about his suit was uncalled for, but since Bret was leaving the business, he didn't care what they said. He didn't need Max anymore. But then Max knocked what Rob was wearing too.

– So, that's it, Max said. – End of an era. After all I've done.

– I'm grateful, Bret said.

– Don't be. I did good off you, Max said. – The easy days are over for you not me.

Feeling liberated, Bret felt he needed to walk off his elation. Tracie offered to go for a walk with him, and they held hands from Max's house to Arlington Point until they were crossing the Maryland Bridge. Tracie looked pretty in pedal pushers and sneakers. In the middle of the bridge they stopped to look down into the Assiniboine River and then up and across at the Cornish Library. Tracie's head was turned just so, and she was smiling at him with her blue, sunlit eyes. They were still holding hands.

– So you're out? Tracie asked.

– I am.

– New suit. New shoes. New life?

– Sure. I'm happy.

He let go of her hand, stooped, pressed his stomach against the railing. Watching and hearing the rushing water gave him vertigo.

– This new life, she said. – That new suit? It's beautiful on you but it makes you look like you're wearing shoes too small for you. You look unhappy. Where are you going in it?

– Synagogue. It's the High Holidays tomorrow. Even the fish in the sea will tremble.

– Fish are stupid. But Max is going with his father. I'd go if he asks me.

– You're not Jewish.

– So?

– He can't marry you, you know.

– We'll see.

– You should leave him.

– He was your idea in the first place, she said. – You handed me off to him.

– We were broken up.

– You pushed me.

– I thought you were feeling bad.

– Of course. I was. But you dumped me and you pushed me at Max.

She joined him, pressing her body against the rail, clasping it with two hands, looking down into the water.

– You like Max, he said.

– Everybody likes him.

– But now you know he's not for you.

– You're stupid.

– I'm going with a friend and her family, Bret said. – To synagogue tomorrow.

– To tremble?

– I haven't been for years. Maybe I will do some trembling tomorrow.

– What friend?

– Just a friend.

– A girlfriend?

– My fiancée.

Her face caved in and she let go of the rail with one hand to cover a gasp. Her bottom lip started trembling, and her eyes filled with tears. Finally, she managed to say:

– Is she rich?

– Not as much as I had imagined. But pretty rich.

– Is that the thing you were working on? To become a parasite? That's why you're leaving Max?

– You should leave him, too.

Now she could look at him, angrily, contemptibly, because she was pissed off.

– You're a suck, she said.

– I'm in love with her.

– What about me? Look at me.

She moved to kiss him and he moved away. Then he bent his head down.

– Look at me! – I was pretending that night with Terri. Pretending I wasn't jealous.

– I don't want you.

She shoved him. She grabbed his chin so that he'd look at her but he pulled away. She squeezed his hand tight until his knuckles cracked and he turned his head until their eyes met again.

– You're hurting me, he said.

– You're hurting me with what you're saying.

He'd felt her hurt; she didn't have to say it. She was lost and dark to him so he didn't feel as bad for her as he had expected, because, he thought, like all sucks and upstarts, that his feelings were more important than the feelings of those he was leaving behind.

He wrenched his hand free and dashed for the other side of the bridge, to a view of the west side of the city and a sunset high as the moon.

– Don't judge yourself too harshly! she called after him.

He kept running all the way back to Arlington Point, where he skidded to avoid stumbling and flying face first into the river.

Bent over, panting, his chest hot and painful, hands on knees, he thought that another part of his life had been put in order, and the thought calmed him: his promises and punishments and rewards were in a new balance. He would never see Max or Tracie or Rob again; that was his new promise. This was his real start in life, and he would be pure and keep his promises. After he married and bought that cottage for his mother, he'd drift away from her and from Carl; in their place would be Sandra, and Mr. and Mrs. Sugarman, and Adara, and Abe, and the Shriners, and the monkeys, of course, and the mouse pressed flat into the bale of cloth.

Thighs and calves aching, he walked back to his car parked in front of Max's and drove home. He skipped supper and climbed into his childhood bed for the first time that summer, with a wretched headache, and slept for twelve hours.

He slept in till 9:30. He thought it was the radio in the kitchen that finally woke him. Or maybe the clatter of pans or the smell of French toast. The radio from the kitchen reported that the mercury had hit 70. He turned on his transistor radio and tuned in to a blues station while he worried about the day ahead.

Bret knotted his tie and put one arm through his suit jacket sleeve, then the other. His mother had polished his dress shoes. As he pulled the laces tight, he sensed Carl smiling at him from his bedroom door. Bret adored Carl's frank smiles and good moods.

– I didn't know you were back. Where'd you get the suit? Where're you going?

– To *shiel*, Bret said.

– Haven't seen you all summer. It's going to be hot today.

– I told you to come out to the beach. I had an extra room.

– No car. I was busy.

– I'll be back soon. Things are good.

– Why?

– Mom knows. She'll tell you. Did you matriculate?

– Yeah. Which *shiel*? She told me about some girl. You're engaged?

– You can use my car today. I'm cabbing it.

– Okay. There's French toast.

Too apprehensive to wait inside after breakfast, Bret stepped out into the September heat and stood on the sidewalk looking up and down the street under a light-blue sky. It was already 11. He was anxious about how long the cab was taking. He turned his head and nodded to his mother and Carl, who were watching and waving through the picture window. He took one last look at them over his shoulder.

A Yellow cab approached and a hope seized him that it would sail right by. As it slowed he fidgeted; the driver had an arm draped out his open window and a cheek turned to squint at the house numbers. Bret's fingers jittered as the cab pulled up to the curb. The only reason he got in was because he felt his mother's and Carl's eyes on the back of his suit. The driver slapped down the flag on the meter and the fare jumped from $00.00 to $00.25.

Each snap of the meter was like a jab to his heart, striking deeper and sharper as they neared his destination. After they crossed the bridge southbound the Sugarmans' stylish synagogue appeared. An actual bead of sweat broke and slid slowly down his back. He rolled down his window for air, bracing himself on their approach, feeling trapped.

As the cab drew up to the synagogue it was slowed by two lanes of large cars trimmed with sparkling chrome dropping off the latecomers, mostly women looking stunning in suits and heels and hats, some wearing their fur coats, surprising on this beautiful day, others draping theirs over an arm, conversing with friends and acquaintances, or enjoying re-encounters after the summer holidays. At most they would have to sit just an hour inside until the *shofar* blew.

In a chatty group of women he noticed Mrs. Sugarman, ahead of fashion, the only one in a pant-suit, holding a large beige purse by long straps in both hands, partially concealed by her formidable mink coat. She was wearing a matching mink beret. Sandra was standing next to her in a dress with zany black and grey squares with a collar that looked like a yoke, not the outfit she had modeled for him. She was receiving charming smiles from the group, but her expression looked vague and polite. Bret was no match for them.

Bret thought he would pass out as the cab-meter clicked.

– I can't pull in – there's no space by the curb, the driver said. – Wanna get out here? Is this good enough?

– Drive. A bit further, Bret said, surprised by his own voice. – I'll say when.

Sandra's mother shot a glance at him sitting in the back seat of the creeping cab. She knocked elbows with Sandra to get her attention and when Sandra's head turned Bret met her eyes. As Sandra saw the cab was not braking, her cheeks turned ripe red and her mouth jumped open, then her eyes widened in fascination.

Bret's eyes locked on hers and he turned his shoulders to stare out the back window to watch her shape diminish as she watched him drive on. The two summer lovers exchanged a spark of complicity. As he felt the cab speed up he saw her head turn back to her mother's friends and the last thing Bret was sure he saw was that she had engaged in their conversation. For lack of breath he felt incapable of giving further instructions to the driver, yet he was able to grunt, then inhale sharply, and say:

– Keep driving. Sorry.

ACKNOWLEDGMENTS

I would like to thank:

Rolf Maurer, as always, and the team at New Star Books, Vlad Cristache and Melissa Swann.

And Melva McLean, for how she fixes things in post.